A GRISLY DISCOVERY

He bent over the dead man, ignoring Sara's low voiced, frantic sounding protests. His hand went out. He drew it back with a thin scream.

"What is it?" Sara asked, shuddering.

"I touched something. Something wet." His voice was a whisper. "Sara, turn on the lights."

She stumbled across the room. The room sprang into view, shabby furniture, framed theatrical posters on the walls, books, newspapers—every detail distinct in a hard clear light.

There was a dark stain on the cloth of his waistcoat— and it was still growing.

"It's blood," Sara whispered. "On your hand too."

BANTAM BOOKS offers the finest in classic and modern English murder mysteries. Ask your bookseller for the books you have missed.

Agatha Christie

DEATH ON THE NILE
A HOLIDAY FOR MURDER
THE MYSTERIOUS AFFAIR
  AT STYLES
POIROT INVESTIGATES
POSTERN OF FATE
THE SECRET ADVERSARY
THE SEVEN DIALS MYSTERY
SLEEPING MURDER

Carter Dickson

DEATH IN FIVE BOXES
THE SKELETON IN THE
  CLOCK
THE WHITE PRIORY
  MURDERS

Catherine Aird

HENRIETTA WHO?
HIS BURIAL TOO
A LATE PHOENIX
A MOST CONTAGIOUS GAME
PASSING STRANGE
THE RELIGIOUS BODY
SLIGHT MOURNING
SOME DIE ELOQUENT
THE STATELY HOME
  MURDER

Patricia Wentworth

THE FINGERPRINT
THE IVORY DAGGER
THE LISTENING EYE
MISS SILVER COMES TO
  STAY
POISON IN THE PEN
SHE CAME BACK
THROUGH THE WALL

Elizabeth Lemarchand

BURIED IN THE PAST
DEATH ON DOOMSDAY

Margaret Erskine

THE FAMILY AT
  TAMMERTON
NO. 9 BELMONT SQUARE
THE WOMAN AT
  BELGUARDO

Margaret Yorke

CAST FOR DEATH
DEAD IN THE MORNING
GRAVE MATTERS

Ruth Rendell

A DEMON IN MY VIEW
THE FALLEN CURTAIN
A SLEEPING LIFE

June Thomson

ALIBI IN TIME
CASE CLOSED
THE LONG REVENGE

E. X. Ferrars

ALIVE AND DEAD
EXPERIMENT WITH DEATH
FROG IN THE THROAT
LAST WILL AND TESTAMENT
MURDERS ANONYMOUS

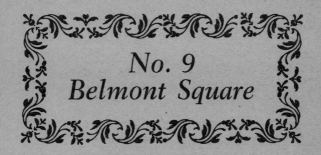

No. 9 Belmont Square

Margaret Erskine

BANTAM BOOKS
TORONTO · NEW YORK · LONDON · SYDNEY

All of the characters in this book are fictitious, and
any resemblance to actual persons, living or dead, is
purely coincidental.

*This low-priced Bantam Book
has been completely reset in a type face
designed for easy reading, and was printed
from new plates. It contains the complete
text of the original hard-cover edition.*
NOT ONE WORD HAS BEEN OMITTED.

NO. 9 BELMONT SQUARE

*A Bantam Book / published by arrangement with
Doubleday & Company, Inc.*

PRINTING HISTORY
Doubleday edition published June 1963
Bantam edition / October 1982

ISBN 0-553-22827-7

Published simultaneously in the United States and Canada

---

*Bantam Books are published by Bantam Books, Inc. Its trademark,
consisting of the words "Bantam Books" and the portrayal of a rooster,
is Registered in U.S. Patent and Trademark Office and in other countries.
Marca Registrada. Bantam Books, Inc., 666 Fifth Avenue, New York,
New York 10103.*

PRINTED IN THE UNITED STATES OF AMERICA

O   0 9 8 7 6 5 4 3 2 1

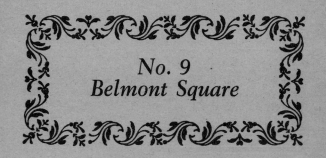

No. 9
Belmont Square

Chapter 1

It was strange that so many people who were later to be involved in the case of the Hungarian singer saw the programme "Out of the Past" only by chance.

Septimus Finch would not have seen it had it not been for his sergeant, Archie Slater. He did not like opera, and certainly he did not want an opera singer screeching in his ear—even on the expensive new television set which he had had installed to replace his old one.

He would have made some excuse had not that young man confided in him that Istvan Kardos had always been one of his heroes. This had surprised Finch very much. He knew Slater as a lively and irreverent young man, good at poker and a fast rugger wing three quarter. To find in him not only a love of music, but the seed of hero-worship, was intriguing—a bit touching too.

"Tell me when the programme is to be and I'll lay in some drinks," he offered in his gentle drawling voice. He added hopefully, "Who knows? Perhaps the fellow will stir himself up a nice spot of trouble. It isn't everyone who can afford to take a good look at his past in front of several million people."

Slater was shocked. "Istvan Kardos sang in public for forty-two years," he said stiffly. "That's an unprecedented length of time for a tenor. He must have lived for his work and nothing else."

Finch looked at him sadly. The evening promised to be even worse than he had imagined.

He was a large bland man with an air of benign disinterestedness. His walk was deceptively lazy. His voice was soft and light in timbre. He held the rank of Detective Inspector and lived in a flat in a cul-de-sac off Fleet Street. It had the great advantage, in his eyes, of being over a pub, the Black Swan. There he commanded great respect, not so much for being one of Scotland

Yard's best known murder specialists, as because of his participation, one evening, in a beer-drinking contest.

Five days after this conversation saw him and his sergeant
in the flat waiting for the programme to begin. Outside was the
fog and cold of late December, but inside it was warm and
comfortable. Finch sat in one of the deep, low armchairs. His
long legs trailed in front of him, and there was a tankard of beer
in his hand. Since he must suffer, then that suffering should be
mitigated as far as possible.

"I once sat through an opera," he said in reminiscent tones.
"It was called 'The Devil's Bullets.' The two principal characters, I remember, spent the whole time bursting into song about
the evil omens that surrounded them, and bewailing the darkness
of their future. There was a whole lot of stage thunder and green
lightning. It was then that the chap I was after tried to make his
getaway. If he'd had any sense he'd have got up and burst into
song about the evil omens that darkened *his* future. As it was I
nabbed him in the foyer and Mr. Justice Lavery gave him seven
years for fraudulent conversion."

" 'The Devil's Bullets' is one of Von Weber's best known
operas," said Slater seriously. "I never cared much for it. Now
take . . ."

But what Slater was about to take remained, somewhat to
his superior's relief, unrevealed. The signature tune of "Out of
the Past" rolled out. The name of the programme flashed onto
the screen. The announcer explained the central idea, and Istvan
Kardos stepped into the limelight—and stayed there.

He was a short man, very round and stocky. He had a flat,
high-cheek-boned face, a wide frog's mouth, prominent heavy-
lidded eyes, and a mass of tiny laughter lines. Whether the
laughter was always—or even usually—kindly was problemati-
cal. He had a strong compelling personality which he had no
difficulty in projecting to his audience, both seen and unseen.

Finch, who had expected to be bored, found his attention
held by the sheer entertainment value of the programme. Fascinated, too, by the character of Istvan Kardos himself, so different from what Archie had led him to expect.

At first he put him down as a plump voluptuary. Then he
saw that there was more to the little man than that. Underneath
the clowning, the bonhomie and gallantry there was something
tough, ruthless. That mouth, when it was not smiling——? The
lively intelligent eyes, too, could hold a chilling light.

The programme was on the Third Channel. It owed some-

thing to the sound programme "Where Are You Now?" and still
more to the television one "This Is Your Life." It took its
course with a little more sentiment and a great deal more animation than was usual.

Singers, conductors, even a displaced Austrian nobleman,
appeared. Kardos remembered them all. There was a great deal
of hand-shaking. Kissing was not confined to the women—of
whom there were many.

There were tales of triumphant first nights, of wild enthusiasm and endless curtain calls. Everyone seemed delighted to see
everyone else. Items of news were exchanged. There were jokes
about the English way of life. Some of them must have been
unscripted, for the compere's smile grew a little fixed.

"That fellow's getting a slightly hunted look," Finch commented. "If he doesn't take care, the programme is going to
over-run its time."

Slater did not seem to hear him, so lost was he to his
surroundings.

Now Kardos had come to his solo part. The stage had been
cleared. Again he took command. His warm musical voice, with
its attractive foreign intonation, wove a dream. His strong, square
hands, no less than his mobile features, emphasised every fleeting nuance of expression. He looked straight out of the screen
and took the viewers into his confidence.

He had, he said, given a great deal of thought to the
question of who it was whom he would like to meet again. And,
perhaps, because to the old the far distance was clearer than the
middle—or perhaps because at heart he was a sentimental fellow, his mind had gone back to the romance of his youth, when
all the world was young and peace had seemed the natural state
of man.

He had been about to make his debut at the Vienna Opera
House in Puccini's "La Bohème." The girl had had the part of
Musetta, a grisette. She had been a beautiful young creature, a
Russian, and he had loved her madly. He had thought that she
loved him in return. Why should she not? He was young, gay,
prepossessing and with a great future in front of him. (His
expression, his intonation both said, "Ah, the self-assurance and
conceit of youth!")

"My days passed in a veritable—what shall I say?—a
veritable *miasma* of happiness. Then came the opening night. It
was a magnificent house, uniforms, decorations, bare shoulders,
fans and jewels. Ah, those jewels! They were to lose me my lady

love, my incomparable Tamara. She was lured away by an archduke, the dashing, elegant and wicked nobleman of tradition and story book.

"He took a fancy to my sweetheart and she took a fancy to his possessions. She was lost to me. Lost to the world of song. She became the toast of Vienna. She rode in a carriage, flowers and feathers in her bonnet. And, when she was alone, no doubt she took out those bright emblems of the archduke's infatuation.

"There was one in particular I remember. A single flawless diamond known as the Lake of Fire. How can I ever forget it? Brilliant, scintillating, ice-cold and yet burning at the heart." And somehow his face and fingers managed to express the wonder of the stone so that there was something electric in the air—or was it that the audience found the emotion within themselves?

"A jewel," Kardos confided, "is like a lover. It entertains, captivates and satisfies. It is best enjoyed in solitude. A solitude *à deux* you understand. It gets under the skin so that one becomes obsessed with it. To be parted from it would be to lose the meaning of life. And so it was with little Tamara and the Lake of Fire."

Later Finch was to think that it was then that Murder stepped onto the stage, unperceived by the man whose words had called it up.

"As for me," Kardos continued, "I—well, I did the equivalent of going to shoot wild beasts in Africa. I took my broken heart to the United States of America, to the Metropolitan Opera House. There I again sang the part of Rodolfo in 'La Bohème.' And there I had an overwhelming success. The critics were unanimous. Mr. Kardos sang, not only superbly, but with the greatest of feeling.

"I had not been long in America when an archduke—not alas, my rival—was assassinated at Serajevo. War swept away the world I had known and Tamara with it. Years later I was back in that sad, dismembered Austria. I enquired, I searched. Not for love you understand but, well, I told you that I am a sentimental fellow. I could get no news of my faithless sweetheart. No one knew. No one cared. In the ruin of a nation what was one lovely woman?

"I never heard of her again. Never knew what became of her but at times, through the years, the vision of Tamara would rise up before me, making other loves seem a little insipid, chill, ordinary. And now, since passion is spent and I am old and, to the old, the greatest happiness lies in shared memories, I say—no, I implore—Tamara Lubova come out of the past.''

The deep musical voice ceased. For a moment of time the bright compelling eyes gazed out with a warmly expectant air. Then the picture dissolved, the names of those concerned began to roll into sight—guests, compere, producer . . .

The programme was over.

In the comfortable fire-lit room there was silence for a moment. Finch got up and switched off the set.

Slater drew a deep breath. ''He was just as I'd imagined him—a great singer and a great man.''

Finch looked at him with amusement. Opera certainly had a bemusing effect. ''But hardly the ascetic of your imagination?''

''Oh, I don't know, sir. Most tenors are plump. It's glands as a rule, not self-indulgence.''

''And there was I thinking of the thousands of good meals he must have eaten. The hundreds of women he must have made love to. Not,'' Finch added thoughtfully, ''that I thought him soft. In fact, he reminded me of a mechanical dancing mouse I had as a child. It was covered in velvet, I remember, soft and pleasing to the touch. It was only on further investigation that I found it had an unyielding metal foundation.''

Slater seemed to emerge from a hero-worshipping reverie. ''You didn't like the programme?'' he asked incredulously.

''I found it very interesting,'' said Finch solemnly. He could not resist the temptation to pull his sergeant's leg.

''But something was wrong?''

''I was just wondering what would happen if Tamara Lubova were to accept that invitation.''

Slater laughed. ''Not much chance of that, I'm afraid.''

Finch looked at him. ''You don't have to be afraid, Archie. But what of Tamara? Don't you think she must have cause to be afraid?''

Slater stared. ''I see what you mean.'' And then, ''But look here, sir,'' he protested, ''the chances against her still being alive—in this country—seeing the programme—must be astronomical.''

''And against anyone who knows her being in the country and seeing the programme?'' said Finch, busily embroidering the theme. ''I tell you, Archie, I never heard a plainer invitation to murder. This clot, Kardos, gave the woman's name, Tamara Lubova. And, with her name, her nationality—Russian. And to sew it up he practically guaranteed that the diamond would still be in her possession."

"I should hardly call Istvan Kardos a clot," said Slater coldly. "And if he were a bit indiscreet, with conditions as they were after the First World War the woman must have been forced to sell her jewellery to live."

"Her lesser jewels, yes. The Lake of Fire, no. Kardos was right there. The passion for a jewel can be like a miser's passion for gold. And you don't need me to tell you how often the coroner holds an inquest on some old biddy who's died of malnutrition with a fortune hidden away in the very room in which she died."

"Wonder what the stone's worth?" The police officer was beginning to triumph over the opera lover. Even so Slater would not admit, even to himself, that his hero might have done more than drop a clanger.

Finch answered his question with another. "How many diamonds, do you think, achieve the distinction of having a name?"

"Offhand I can think of the Star of the East, the Liberator, the Koh-in-Noor. . . ." He broke off with a little yelp of dismay. "Sorry, sir, but I just remembered. Wasn't a diamond recently withdrawn at Sotheby's at £125,000?"

Finch looked at him. "Odd that you should have mentioned that particular stone because it, too, once belonged to the Hapsburgs. Still," he added, "no need to panic. Let's stick to something moderate as the value of the Lake of Fire. Say— £20,000?"

He got up. He took his tankard and that of his guest over to where a small beer barrel stood supported on wooden wedges. Slater watched him, frowning a little. Finch was known to have an instinct for impending crime. It amounted almost to a sixth sense. But this time he was wrong. He must be wrong. "If Kardos couldn't find her in Vienna, I expect it was because she had gone back to Russia."

"She wouldn't do that. Russia was in the throes of revolution. The world of pleasure as Tamara Lubova knew it had gone from there too."

"I seem to have heard that Paris was the place where most of the White Russians settled."

"Come," said Finch in high good humour at the course the conversation had taken, "that's better. And the last war would have moved her on again—to London. With the Germans there

Paris would have been no place for a frivolous creature like Tamara.''

Slater moved irritably. "But the whole thing's absurd. Incredible—a pipe dream.''

"I said *if* Tamara Lubova showed up. If—if! If the millionth chance came off, what then?''

"The old girl might find herself in a pretty nasty position," Slater admitted reluctantly.

"Exactly." Finch came back with two brimming tankards. "After this evening's performance she'll be in danger if anyone can identify her. She'll be in danger if anyone knows where she is. And most of all she'll be in danger if she gets in touch with Istvan Kardos.''

"Oh, come off it, sir. I mean—you can't seriously suggest that an elderly, wealthy and prominent figure like Istvan Kardos would covet an old woman's jewels?''

Finch took a long drink. "In the unlikely event of Tamara Lubova getting herself murdered," he said firmly, "I should put our friend, Kardos, first on the list of suspects.''

"But he would scarcely have been as forthcoming with his information if he'd had a possible theft in mind." Slater, half convinced, was fighting a rearguard action.

"There're two answers to that," said Finch, relenting. "The first, that, like you, he considers the chance of Tamara turning up to be so slight as not to be worth considering. The other, that neither the diamond nor the lady have any existence outside of his imagination. They were just something he'd dreamed up to touch the great big heart of the British Public!''

"In that case, sir," said Slater, "what are we arguing about?''

Only when their pleasant and mildly convivial evening was over Finch walked to the window and drew back the curtain. He stood there looking out. Suppose he, Finch, had been right after all? Suppose that she was somewhere out there, this lady in the dark? This fascinating trollop of Kardos' description? An old woman now, with perhaps a lifetime of sin and intrigue and concealment behind her—but still no match for her onetime lover.

But it had been only a flight of fancy. It went from his mind now, tenuous as the mist that had gathered in the street below. He turned from the window. A shame really to have teased Archie like that.

*   *   *

Istvan Kardos looked sourly at his correspondence sent on to his flat in St. John's Wood from the television studios. He had had letters from old colleagues who had not appeared on the programme but had seen it. Letters from admirers who had heard him at the height of his fame. There were, too, those which he had come to call the Tamara letters—and no one could have been more astonished than he when the first of them had arrived.

He was not a nice man. He did not want to be known as a nice man but his success was dear to him. For this reason he had given great thought to his television appearance. The story of his lost love and her romance with the Austrian archduke had seemed perfect. It had romance, colour, even a touch of naughtiness. He had never thought of Tamara Lubova seeing his programme. Far less that she might accept his invitation to "come out of the past."

At the first sight of the signature he had felt a great surge of excitement, covetousness and greed. Alas! A glance at the letter had shown him that the writer was an impostor.

Since then he had had fifteen letters all purporting to come from Tamara Lubova. All written in varying tones of affection. All suggesting a meeting and all, he supposed, from neurotic love-starved or insane females.

He carried the new batch of correspondence into the sitting room of his flat. He sank into a chair and, with a golden penknife shaped like a fish, the gift of an admirer, slit the most expensive looking of the envelopes. "Dear Mr. Kardos," he read, "as a lover of opera and a great admirer of your voice it gave me great pleasure. . . ." blah, blah, blah . . . and not even an invitation to a meal. The next letter was from a fellow singer. He angered Kardos by alluding to "us two old men." His letter followed the first into the wastepaper basket.

At the third letter the lines of annoyance faded. The prominent eyes stared. The lips mouthed a soundless "So!"

It was typed, badly typed, even to the signature. Typed on a single sheet of writing paper from which the address had been cut. It began abruptly, without salutation or any form of address.

It is many years since I heard the name Tamara Lubova. Now I write to tell you that the person you mentioned is dead and wishes to remain so. Do not speak of her again. So that you will know that this letter is genuine I sign it with the name you know her by, and in the way you know.

Lubova, Tamara, the Red.

Underneath the signature was written; as if in afterthought, *"The Lake of Fire was sold long ago."*

It was the signature, as much as anything, that convinced Kardos that the letter was genuine, written as it was in the Hungarian manner with the surname first.

Kardos felt in his head a great roaring. His heart pounded. Then caution reasserted itself. It might be another hoax. The letter might not be from Tamara Lubova at all. But wasn't it worth taking seriously? What would that entail? A little thought—brain-work? A little trouble—discomfort perhaps? What was that compared to the possibility—even the remotest possibility—of laying hands on the Lake of Fire!

He had made a great deal of money in his time—and he had spent a great deal. He had enough left to keep him comfortably. But with the stone—— He closed his eyes and a whole vista of extravagant living opened before his mental vision.

It was worth taking the letter at its face value. Worth it a thousand times. From now on the letter *was* genuine—until he had proved it to be false.

As for disposing of the stone—Kardos chuckled to himself. A great many valuables had come out of Hungary since the last war, more since the uprising. He had disposed of quite a number for people who might, or might not, have been their rightful owners. He knew the ropes. The sale, even of the Lake of Fire, would present no difficulty.

There remained then only the problem of identification.

In the far off days to which the letter alluded the word red could have had no connection with communism, but only with the colour of Tamara's hair.

So her hair had been red. Curious that he should have forgotten that. But then the unfortunate fact was that he had forgotten entirely what she looked like.

He sat on, eyes vacant, frowning in an effort to recall the past.

Red Tamara!

Nothing came. No mental picture beyond that of the Vienna Opera House—and then there was no one in it but himself. Himself and—yes, of all the infuriating things. The only figure he could recall was that of the great Russian soprano, Sinada Jursewskaya.

Kardos drummed a finger on his forehead in exasperation. Had Tamara been short or tall? He had always disliked singing with people who were taller than himself. Taller that is, when he was wearing built-up heels. So probably she had been shorter than he. Or, at any rate, no taller. But then again, in bed a woman's height was of little importance—and he had been her lover. Of that he *was* certain. He would have had no interest in her otherwise, for she had had neither influence nor fortune.

Tamara? How had she been in bed? Ach! Of what use to remember that? He dismissed this aspect of their relationship impatiently. It was some means of identification that he required. A mole, a characteristic gesture, the colour of her eyes, the shape and set of her ears.

With an exclamation of angry impatience he sprang to his feet. Set himself walking to and fro, his gaze abstracted, his step light, cat-like.

He subjected himself to a mental catechism.

Her eyes? He could not remember.

Her complexion? Unknown.

Her figure? Plump? He liked them plump. Most singers tend to be plump but now, why she must be nearly seventy. She may be gross, skinny but youthfully plump? No.

Her temperament? It must surely have matched her hair—but that was a long time ago. Fire dies—as memories die. At least as far as he was concerned. That *she* remembered *him* occasioned him no surprise. There had been many women in his life. And to be loved by him was, he felt, an experience not to be forgotten.

"Tamara," he said aloud. "Tamara, the Red." And then, as if by so doing he would force a mental picture of the woman, "Tamara Lubova," he cried in a loud voice. But nothing came to him. Neither ghost nor echo of a voice.

There remained then only the letter itself to serve as a link.

He snatched up the envelope. It was greyish green and square. The postmark was Seamarsh. He had never been there but he remembered that it was a small old-fashioned seaside resort with a cross-channel service to France.

He walked over to a bookcase and took down an R.A.C. book. It was an old one, going back to the days when he had owned a large handsome car and a chauffeur to drive it.

There it was. Seamarsh (Sussex) population 12,037. London 64 miles.

He replaced the book and took up the letter. The paper matched the envelope. It was not of a very good quality yet, obviously, it had had a printed or engraved address. This suggested either a small hotel or a boarding house. Or perhaps—Kardos made a grimace—a charitable institution, such as an old people's home.

His first impulse was to pack a suitcase and set off for Seamarsh. A moment's reflection showed him a more satisfactory course. He would not go looking for the writing paper. He would first try and make it come to him.

He would write to the hotels listed in the R.A.C. book. If that did not bring him the address he wanted he would write to the Seamarsh Town Council telling them that he had heard of their so healthy and pleasant town, and asking them if they would be kind enough to send him addresses of places suitable for an elderly fellow like himself to pass his last days.

He had no doubt but that he would get an answer. The English are a polite race. Semi-illiterate natives from the wilds of Africa could write for catalogues of machinery they could not afford to buy and could not work if they did buy. And teenagers could apply to the Ritz or the Dorchester from obscure Italian villages for luggage stickers. Or from Iceland for seeds that could not be grown there anyway—and always they gôt the polite reply.

"As for the Town Council of Seamarsh when they see that my request is so reasonable," he told himself, "that I require only a list of hotels and guest houses, they will be so relieved that they will compile and send it off immediately."

The replies from the hotels listed in the R.A.C. book brought no result. And at first the replies from the lesser hotels and boarding houses, whose addresses had been supplied by the Town Council, were no more successful.

"Good cooking." . . . "South aspect." . . . "Separate tables." Bah! It was not this that he looked for. Then he sat very still, staring down at the envelope in his hand. It was greyish green in colour and square in shape.

Hurriedly he slit it open. He drew out the letter inside. It, too, was greyish green. The water mark was identical with that on the original paper. It was of the correct width and the address was printed.

"No. 9 Belmont Square, Seamarsh, Sussex."

The writing was firm and, he judged, hurried, as if the writer had other, more pressing, matters to attend to. His eyes ran over the words.

> *"Homely"* . . . *"part of the house closed for the winter"* . . . *"no central heating"* . . . *"plain but good cooking"* . . . *"very welcome but fear you will not be comfortable."*

It was signed, "Yours faithfully, Sara Harkness."

Kardos sat looking at the letter in silence for a time. He made a wry face. "I too," he murmured sadly, "I too do not think that I will be comfortable."

Septimus Finch was thinking of going down to the canteen for lunch. Three weeks had passed and the television appearance of Istvan Kardos had gone from his mind. Or, at least, lingered only as a slightly guilty memory.

He looked up as Archie Slater burst into the small room he called his own. "He's gone," he cried, coming to a dramatic halt, his back to the door. "And I was so certain in my own mind that it was all rot." He frowned worriedly. "And then to hear he'd done a bunk. It seemed the end."

Finch returned to his papers. "I'm like that myself," he murmured. "I get madly excited when I find some unidentified person has gone from an address I don't know to a destination I can't guess at."

Slater took a deep breath. He grinned reluctantly. "Sorry, sir. Of course, you're not with me. But it's Kardos who's gone. Istvan Kardos. Disappeared from his flat not fifteen minutes ago."

"What?" Abruptly Finch jerked himself upright. "Oh, my ears and whiskers! Why didn't you say so before?"

"I know. I was a bit upset. But anyway I've only just heard." Slater moved towards where Finch sat at his desk. Silently Finch pointed to a chair. "It was like this, sir. I knew that you had the reputation for recognising almost the birth of a crime. But this time I felt certain that you were wrong—and I set out to prove it. I mean . . . Istvan Kardos! I can scarcely believe it now."

Finch wagged a sympathetic head. All things considered he could scarcely believe it either. "Perhaps the fellow's had a sudden call to his old mother's death bed."

"If he had," Slater retorted gloomily, "he went a queer way about it." He added with a solemnity that increased Finch's sense of guilt, "After what you said I looked up Kardos' address in the telephone book. Then I hung about the block of flats until I saw the porter come out. I followed him to the local and got into conversation. I . . . well, I know I shouldn't have done it." He looked appealingly at his superior. "That's what makes it so jolly awkward now."

"You told him you were a police officer and that you wanted a watch kept on Kardos, and to let you know immediately if he went away?"

"That's about the size of it," Slater admitted unhappily. He could read nothing into Finch's expression which had remained as bland as a Chinaman's. "He agreed to ring me up if anything interesting happened. Well," he took a deep breath, "he telephoned me just now. Said that Kardos suddenly appeared from the lift. Told him to stop his milk and newspapers as he would be away for an indefinite time and then just walked off—as he was."

One of Finch's eyebrows climbed. "No luggage?"

"No, sir. But his pockets were bulging."

"And that, for such a natty gentleman as our Mr. Kardos, must have meant something."

"You don't think," Slater ventured hopefully, "that it meant he'd soon be back—his having no luggage I mean?"

Finch shook his head. "Not he. Razor and intimate personal belongings in his pockets. The rest left ready in some railway cloakroom to be picked up. Trouble is we don't know which railway station."

Not that Finch seemed distressed at the thought. Indeed his expression was of simple pleasure and wonderment. He might have been contemplating one of the Seven Wonders of the World. The Hanging Gardens of Babylon or perhaps the Colossus of Rhodes. Either way he looked very happy.

"After all," he murmured, "if Kardos is wrong he's lost nothing. If he's right then anything may happen. A diamond like that is pretty certain to mean disaster."

"If it exists."

"It exists all right. I took the trouble to find out. It even has a history. It was given by Catherine, the Great, to a member of a cadet branch of the Hapsburgs. A handsome fellow who was believed, not unnaturally, to have been her lover. The Lake of Fire had been a family heirloom right up to the time the then archduke gave it to his mistress, Tamara Lubova. The diamond merchant I spoke to about it was an Austrian. An old man. He remembers the scandal it caused."

Slater sighed. So much for wishful thinking. "Anyway," he said, thankfully, "if Kardos does get in a mess, it won't be anything to do with us."

Finch looked affronted. "You get on with your work, young

Archie. Otherwise I may have to report you." He returned to his own work. "Suborning porters indeed!" And some time later in an incensed tone of voice, "And my name next on the rota for an out-of-town assignment!"

Chapter 2

If Istvan Kardos had been reluctant to seek the hospitality of No. 9 Belmont Square, its owner had been equally reluctant to have him there.

To Sara Harkness he represented so many more potatoes to peel, so many more plates to wash, another bed to make. Overwork had made her short tempered and impatient and now she cursed him roundly.

She was twenty-seven, an angular, young woman who had come to care nothing for her appearance. Whose highest hope was to get through the day without disaster or upset and so crawl exhausted into bed to recoup the strength that would enable her to get through the next day—and the next.

It was difficult now to believe that five years before No. 9 had seemed the answer to her besetting problem. How to make a home for her brother Alan. Rescue him from his gloomy attic bedroom in the Earls Court district of London, and so fulfil her promise to their dead mother.

Their father had died when they were very young. Their mother when Sara had been nineteen and Alan two years younger. She had loved both her children but her son had been her idol. Her last thought had been for his welfare.

"When I'm gone, Sara, you'll have no home," she had said with laboring breath. And it had been true for she had lived on a pension that would cease with her death. "Try and make one for Alan. Give him his chance. He's so gifted, so brilliant. Don't let poverty hold him back."

And Sara, adoring her handsome brother, had determined to do just that. Some way must be found of freeing him from anxiety. Making a home for him. Giving him the loving care and encouragement that was due to his genius.

Her own job on the staff of a well known woman's journal,

15

her gift for looking at old problems in a new and amusing light, seemed of no importance when weighed in the balance with Alan's career on the stage.

It was a career that had progressed from that of Assistant General Manager at the Bankside Theatre to General Understudy when Sara in the early spring of 1957 had the letter that had changed the course of her life and brought the two of them to No. 9 Belmont Square.

It was from the firm of Harkness & Carron, Solicitors, of Seamarsh, Sussex. It told her that their only remaining relative— and that only by marriage—Mrs. Millicent Harkness, widow of the late Geoffrey Harkness, was dead. And that she had left her entire estate, roughly a thousand pounds, her house and its contents, to the girl.

There was one condition. It was that she continue to run the place for a period of twelve months as a guest house for the benefit of the present boarders, and on the same terms as in the past. *"The said twelve months being sufficient to enable the said boarders to find other accommodation."*

This letter had been followed by a personal one from Mr. Carron himself. In it he had recalled that her cousin, the late Geoffrey Harkness, had been his partner and dear friend for over forty years and that he had had the privilege of continuing that friendship with his widow. And that if she, Sara, did decide to accept the legacy, then he hoped that she would allow him to be her friend also. Perhaps even, considering the difference in their ages, to stand in *loco parentis*.

He had asked her to think seriously before deciding to take on the responsibility of No. 9, pointing out that, since Mrs. Harkness had taken in paying guests, not from necessity, but because her husband's death had left her lonely, the guests were of her generation and that their care was a responsibility which, once assumed, would be difficult to relinquish.

Later Sara was to appreciate the force of his warning; for after twelve months not one of the residents of No. 9 had been able to find other lodgings at a price that they could afford. Nor had she had the heart to turn them out, for who else would show them kindness? They were so helpless, so aggravating, so—daft. It was one of the dismaying factors of her position that, as Mr. Carron had foreseen, she had come to accept responsibility for them. Even to grow fond of them. And to the old ladies had been added a fourth guest, a Mr. Gadsby. He had written a few days after she had taken possession of No. 9 to know whether he might return temporarily. Once installed he had, like the others, become a fixture.

But all that was in the future. At the time no thought of refusing the legacy entered her mind. She and her brother had been jubilant. They had never met Mrs. Harkness, nor her husband, and so could not grieve for them. They were rich, independent, householders. They even had a faithful retainer in the person of Daisy Apps, maidservant at No. 9 for nearly thirty years. She had been away ill when they had first taken up residence but had returned soon after.

From then on, dour, stubborn, she had fought Sara's battles, with the old people, with the tradespeople. She would have done it with Alan himself if Sara would have allowed it. Restoring order out of the chaos into which the old ladies' vagaries and Sara's inexperience had thrown it.

By the end of the twelve months they had not felt so rich but the future still looked rosy. Alan was making his first appearance as juvenile lead in the West End. Sara still found time to write an occasional article. The two of them were still going about together and in the summer No. 9 had been gay, full of their friends, coming and going in an unending stream. In the second summer Sara had found it necessary to replace them largely with guests who paid.

In the autumn of the second year things had improved still further. A niece of Mr. Carron's had come to live at No. 9. Rich, beautiful and spoilt, she had recently lost her husband. To Sara she had seemed more aggrieved by her loss than heartbroken.

She had chosen two of the best rooms and a bathroom, for all of which she paid generously. She had seemed in no way put out by the heavy Victorian furniture, the ugly oil paintings on the walls, the depressing covers and curtains. She had asked if she might re-arrange the rooms. Alter them a little. It was only later that Sara realised how far the alterations had gone. How many pieces had been replaced by more attractive bits from other parts of the house.

She was, Sara discovered, an expert at getting what she wanted sweetly but firmly. The trouble was, that after a while, the firmness was what you noticed. Sara wondered whether Harry Brooks had noticed it, whether perhaps he had been a man who did not take kindly to coercion. That would have been hard on Magda. But then it would have been hard on Harry too.

The third and fourth year passed. In spite of the fact that more and more money was coming in they were no better off.

Alan was extravagant, foolish, easily influenced. Sara would not have that it was more than this. And she had promised their mother. . . .

She worked harder, went out less. Without Mr. Carron's friendship and Daisy's devotion and unfailing passion for work, she could not have managed.

Now, on the eve of Istvan Kardos' arrival, she was preparing the evening meal. Working in the large, old-fashioned kitchen with the haphazard efficiency of one forced by circumstances to do something for which she was temperamentally unfitted. Her long legs covered the floor and her rangy height made it easy for her to reach pots and pans.

For all that she was behind with her work. She had been hindered by one of the boarders, Mrs. McGee. Squeak, squeak her bath-chair had sounded along the passage, like a querulous complaining voice.

There had followed Mrs. McGee's own voice, hoarse, confused. Tears had rolled down the hard red cheeks and the grey cropped hair had looked more than ever like a wig.

It was a scene that had been re-enacted so often in the past five years that Sara had ceased really to listen. Her responses had become purely automatic.

"It isn't as if she actually tells us what she did," Sara had once complained to her brother. "A great sin she always calls it but then old people do exaggerate so."

"Mrs. McGee doesn't exaggerate," Alan had retorted grinning. "It's quite obvious to me what her sin was. Didn't her husband break his neck falling down the stairs here? Well, there you are! Mrs. McGee reached out from her bath-chair, pushed him with the end of her crutch and whoosh! down he went. Remember how they quarrelled because he wouldn't let her invest their money as she wanted?"

"I remember how terribly upset she was at his death," Sara had retorted.

"And I remember how she enjoyed gambling away everything he'd left, including his life assurance. The Home Health Drug Co., the King John Adventurers of the Wash—I particularly liked that one—the North Sea Oil Discovery Board, until in two years she was down to living on the pension her husband's firm had allowed her. And she couldn't do that if you didn't overlook it when she's forced to forget a week's payment."

The kitchen door opened. Alan came in. Slim, golden haired, he brought with him a rush of cold air from the passage outside, and a feeling of life and gaiety. The shabby room seemed to be lighted up by the mere fact of his entry.

Sara slipped a lemon meringue pie, destined for tomorrow's lunch, into the oven before she rose to her feet. "Did you get it?"

"Get what? Oh, the job? No, as a matter of fact, by the time I got there the part was filled."

Sara stared at him unbelievingly. She felt her smile of welcome grow stiff on her face. "How d'you mean? By the time you got there? You left here in plenty of time."

"I got there in plenty of time." Alan chose an apple from a dish and bit into it. "There were about ten of us." He perched himself on a corner of the kitchen table, one elegant leg swinging. He fixed his brilliant blue eyes on Sara. "Suddenly the big man's secretary appeared and told us that the part had been filled." He added airily, "There was a lot of talk I can tell you. One of the chaps said he supposed the current pet had got it. You know the old man's reputation."

The thought came into Sara's mind, he's lying. When he stares like that he's lying. She said bitterly, "I suppose the truth is that you went in for a drink somewhere and arrived too late. Or perhaps you met a girl friend and never kept the appointment at all."

"You needn't speak like that." Alan sounded aggrieved. "It's only a few weeks ago I finished that television serial."

"It's exactly five months." Sara spoke through her teeth. Anger and—yes, resentment—seemed to be choking her. "I suppose what you mean is that you still have some of the money left. Well, you'd better make the most of it because it's the last you'll get from that particular source."

Alan looked up. "What d'you mean? I've seen some of the shots and I'm a real heart-throb in them."

"That may be but Mrs. Brooks happens to know the producer. He told her that you behaved reasonably well until they'd filmed half of the scenes. After which you turned up later and later and were more and more tiresome. He said that since it was impossible to write you out of the script, he was only sorry that it wasn't a 'whodunit' so that he could have arranged for you to be the murderer's next victim and get rid of you that way!"

"The woman's a liar."

Sara shrugged. "Mrs. Brooks says the word has gone out that you're not to be employed again in the I.C.O. studios."

Alan threw the core of his apple accurately into the grate.

"Oh well, their pictures were lousy anyway. Still, it's a bit of a bind. The studios are comparatively near."

"I wish you'd think less of your comfort and more of your career. You know quite well that when I inherited this place I was only going to run it until you'd made your name as an actor." She added bitterly. "That was five years ago and all that's happened since is that manager and producers are getting sick of your unreliability."

"Quoting Mrs. Brooks again I suppose." Under the long gold-tipped lashes Alan's eyes were cold. What had come over Sara? He had been pleased with himself when he had come in. He had had a good day in London—even if he hadn't found time to keep that appointment but first his sister and then Magda Brooks had spoilt it all. But he'd get even with the widow now and with Sara later. He said aloud, "How that woman hates me."

Sara was grating cheese. She did not trouble to look up. "Why should she do that?"

"Because—well——" He made a show of hesitation. Then his dazzling smile broke out again. "It's too silly really but she—well, she made a pass at me. You know, sort of Potiphar's wife stuff, only without Potiphar. I—I was probably ungallant." He seemed to be considering. "Yes, I suppose I was. But, my dear, the whole thing took me by surprise. She's so old! And not my style at all."

"She's thirty-four." Sara spoke automatically. So that's why she's always saying things about Alan, she thought. Beastly woman. She did not doubt her brother's story for she knew that to some women he was irresistible. "I'd never have thought she was like that. She always seems so aloof and self-sufficient."

"Madly so," Alan agreed. "Still, she's bound to get temperamental at times. It's three years since her husband died in South Africa. And three years can seem an awful long time."

"Well, she's not going to get temperamental here," said Sara briskly. "I'll ask her to go when she pays her next week's bill."

"My dear girl, for goodness sake don't make a thing out of it. It all happened last summer. She's rather tended to ignore my presence since then."

"Yes, I'd noticed that."

Alan smiled charmingly. "There you are then. No harm's done and, heaven knows, I bear the fair widow no ill feeling."

Sara nodded. "Perhaps you're right. We should certainly

miss her money.'' She looked into the bread bin. "Oh damn! I quite forgot that we needed more bread. Now I shall have to go out after dinner and knock on Dunn's side door for some more.''

"Bad luck," said Alan in his agreeable voice. He did not offer to go himself. It did not occur to him to do so. "Poor old Sara! We should never have come here.''

Sara wiped her forehead with the back of her hand. "You're always saying that, and today, for the first time, I really feel I agree with you. It hasn't helped your career being down here and frankly I wonder how much longer we'll be able to keep going. I haven't been able to pay the interest on the mortgage. The money just isn't there.''

"But old Carron dotes on you. He won't mind.''

"From something he said the other day I think he's beginning to mind. Besides I'm fed up with this life. It's nothing but work, work, work.''

Alan's face assumed a look of charming solicitude. It showed nothing of his anger and dismay. He had got into the habit of blaming his failures on the fact that they lived so far from London, but actually the present set-up suited him admirably. Free bed and board. A place in which to entertain his friends. What money he made his own. (And, by various means, he made a great deal more than his sister supposed.) And Sara only too anxious to martyr herself on his behalf.

He felt aggrieved. Damn all women! Why couldn't they be consistent? He supposed he'd have to pay her some attention. At first he'd given her a lot of his time. Taken her out and about. This had had a twofold advantage. She had paid all the expenses and he had kept her from looking for any other escort, and from the risk of matrimony. Lately she'd been so damned plain that that last danger had seemed past. No, he was safe enough there. After all, she was twenty-seven—and she looked it.

He said aloud, "If you feel like that you just go ahead. You've had a good season and with Magda Brooks and this new chap you'll seem quite prosperous. And, after all," he added, playing what he hoped would be a trump card, "this place does have possibilities. The buyer could easily get a better return for his money by putting up the charges.''

Sara, as he had hoped, took instant alarm. "But the fuddy-duddies can't pay more. What would become of them?''

"They could go into an old people's home.''

"Oh no! They'd be so unhappy.'' Sara could still remember the state they had been in at the end of the first twelve months.

She had not been able to turn them adrift then. How could she do it now when they were four years older, queerer and more helpless? "Besides, what would you do?"

"I'd find somewhere to go," Alan added grinning. "If my stock's down with producers and managers, it's up in other directions."

Said Sara slowly, "I suppose you mean you'd go and live with some girl?"

Alan chuckled. "Better than living with some boy."

The front door bell rang, loud and imperative.

Sara raised her head. "Blast! He's come."

"Sounds like it. What's his name?"

"Mr. Istvan Kardos."

"What?" Alan was staring.

"Mr. Istvan Kardos," Sara repeated. "Alan, how queer you look. Do you know him?"

Said Alan slowly, "Isn't that the name of a celebrated Hungarian opera singer?"

Sara laughed with spontaneous amusement. "What would a celebrated Hungarian opera singer—or for that matter a celebrity of any other nationality—be doing here? No, this must be a poor relation. Or perhaps just a namesake."

Alan laughed too. He looked of a sudden extraordinarily alive and gay. "Of course it's the opera singer! Magda's daft about opera. Always going to Covent Garden. That's where she met him and now he's followed her down here. You'll see! He'll court her madly. Pursuing her by day in spats and patent leather shoes. And at night he'll serenade her, wearing a magnificent dressing gown—no, a silk robe worked with golden dragons, while she flees from him—but not too fast—in a diaphanous peignoir. It's all going to be wildly gay, foreign and intoxicating."

As he spoke, with a few gestures and a change of expression, he seemed first a stout ageing singer and then Magda Brooks, a coy Magda Brooks, with something rather nasty about her.

I suppose that is how she seems to Alan, Sara thought. She could not help laughing but there was an undertone of bitterness. He's so clever. He could get work if he tried, she told herself.

Belmont Square had the depressing look of a district which had gone down in the world. The tall grey double fronted houses were shabby with peeling paint and flaking stucco. Curtains of varying design proclaimed the sad fact that they had been divided into flats. Or, worse still, let off as single rooms.

No. 9 proclaimed its corporate existence by its windows, shrouded first in heavily patterned ecru net and then in silk damask, lined and bobble fringed. It had a bright yellow door painted by Sara in a fit of exuberance when she had first come there to live.

Kardos paid off his taxi. He had banished from his mind any suggestion that the letter might be bogus. To entertain doubts, he knew from experience, was to court failure. Now as he stood in the January dusk, he savoured the peculiar quality of that moment.

The English had a saying that well begun was half done and he had bridged a gap that was half a century old. Caught up on events that had taken place hundreds of miles away—in another country—almost in another life. Five weeks ago Tamara had been but a shadowy figure. Her very name had had to be dredged from the back of his mind. And yet here he was, outside the door of her house.

And what could Tamara do about it? Nothing. She could not complain without explaining the reason for his coming. And to explain was but to risk adding to the number of her enemies.

He chuckled to himself. "No, no, Tamara. You will not speak. This is to be between you and me," he promised himself.

Around him were the small sounds of a town, its working day over and such night life as it had not yet begun. A faint hum of traffic, the sound of the sea in the distance. Across the street the ragged bushes in the square garden rustled in a breath of wind. The footsteps of a solitary walker broke out on the opposite pavement, then died away. And overhead the yellow sodium lighting took all colour from the scene, making it as eerie and weird as any of the operas in which he had figured.

He turned with a flourish and rang the bell, jabbing at it. Imagining it sounding through the decaying house like a trumpet of doom. Terrifying the woman he sought.

The front door was opened by a tall rawboned woman and at once the high note of melodrama was dissipated, lost in the face of her conventional black frock, white apron and cap, her severe eye and air of bleak respectability.

Kardos introduced himself, enjoying his own discomfiture.

"We were expecting you, sir. Come in and I'll show you to your room. Miss Harkness is busy at the moment but she hopes to see you later."

She picked up his suitcase and stood aside for him to enter. She led the way across the hall.

Kardos followed her, their footsteps echoing on the tessellated floor. Bead curtains jingled. Large old pieces of furniture
loomed darkly for the hall was poorly lighted. A fine mahogany
staircase went up in a half circle to a dim landing. The air struck
warm but this was only by contrast with the cold outside. An
appearance of decaying grandeur lay all about him.

"You have a lift?" Kardos asked, surprised. Like everything else in the hall it was ornate with a slightly baroque look
and a lot of tarnished gilt.

"It was put in for the late owner, old Mr. Harkness. This
was a private house in *his* day."

"The world has changed for the worse since then," said
Kardos politely. He fancied that his companion gave the faintest
of sniffs. The ghost of a sniff but very genteel.

She rang for the lift. A whirring noise came from above.
The lift was on its way down.

"You're lucky, sir. The old ladies very often forget to close
the doors, then it stays on their floor."

"The old ladies?" Kardos' voice expressed no more than a
polite interest.

"Four of them—at the top. Quarrelling, gossiping. There
used to be six."

"They died of old age?"

"Old Mrs. Winfield died of heart failure—alone. In this
very lift."

"Horrible!" Kardos shivered involuntarily. He was super-
stitious and it seemed a bad omen.

"The days of man are but as grass."

"Too true." The lift whirled them steadily upwards. "You
have not told me your name?"

"It's Daisy." She spoke shortly.

He nodded. "A charming name." He could not decide
whether her tone had betokened dislike of its incongruity or of the
thought that he should use it. He did not want to antagonise her.

The lift came to a halt. She said abruptly, "You could
move to the top floor if you liked."

"Heaven forbid."

She gave him a repressive glance. "They're big rooms on
this floor. Difficult to heat."

The passage was covered in a red Turkey rug. Kardos,
following the maid's thin ramrod-straight back, took pleasure in
the muffling thickness of the carpet. So much more satisfactory
for his purpose than the hall. He wondered how far it extended.

Daisy opened a door. She walked in and put his suitcase on the luggage rack. "The times of the meals are written up on the wall there. There's a toilet and bathroom almost opposite. For the stairs turn right outside your door. The lift is to the left. If you should want anything you'll have to ask. The bells don't ring."

"Thank you for the information. I can see that we shall get on very nicely together. You look after me and I look after you, yes?"

The words seemed to take Daisy by surprise. A number of emotions flickered over her face, doubt, astonishment, suspicion, and then a sour look of pleasure. Kardos shrugged at the closed door. Did no one here tip?

He turned to look about him curiously. The room was full of dark pieces of mahogany and it was cold. Daisy had been right there. It was cold enough to explain a change to a higher floor should he wish but first he would do a little prospecting. Tamara too—he smiled without mirth—she might try something, friendly or unfriendly, on her own account.

He put some money in the meter and turned the electric fire full on. He washed his hands. Then he paused to read the typed notice put up close to the electric light switch.

> *Breakfast 8.30 to 9 a.m. Luncheon 1 o'clock. Supper 7.30 p.m. Guests are asked to be punctual. Tea served at 4.30 p.m. in the lounge. Please turn off the lights when you leave your room.*

Kardos twisted his long frog's mouth in a grin of appreciation. Very direct and concise, this Miss Harkness. He pictured her as a typical English spinster. The jolly, no nonsense type. High-necked blouses by day and a lot of beads in the evening. And of course, a lover who died. Every elderly self-respecting spinster had a lover who died. Except possibly Daisy. She would have something else. Drink perhaps or religion.

The sound of a gong boomed out, rolling up the stairs and into the room. No good anyone pretending they did not hear that, he reflected. He put it down as another instance of the sound commonsense of this Miss Harkness, whom he felt he knew already.

Swiftly he unpacked his suitcase. Then, opening his door, he turned right down the dimly lighted passage towards the stairs. He reached the corner and halted. He had forgotten to turn the light off on leaving his room. Should he go back? Yes, better so.

He turned. Then he paused, staring, a little thrill of excitement stirring his blood.

A woman had just disappeared through one of the doors. In spite of the improbability he fancied that it was the door to his own room.

Hurriedly, silent on the thick carpet, he retraced his steps. He threw open the door and slipped through almost, it seemed, in one fluid movement.

A little elderly woman was standing, finger on lip, in a contemplative pose before his dressing table. A soft-moving, rather dumpy little woman with a sweet silly expression. Her faded wispy hair was held back by an Alice band of sky blue ribbon. She wore an elaborately ruched pale blue frock with lace on the bodice. Dotted here and there in its complicated folds were little dabs of jewellery—of no particular value as Kardos saw. There were bows on her heelless slippers and numerous narrow gilt bangles on her wrists.

She did not seem at all put out at his entry. "I was just seeing that you had everything," she murmured, gliding towards the door.

"You are Miss Harkness perhaps?"

The faded blue eyes opened very wide. "Oh, no! But I'm a *very* old resident."

Before he had quite realised it she had slipped past him and out of the door. She turned, smiling and bobbing her head in an odd little salute. Then she was gone, moving in the direction of the staircase.

So, Kardos thought, the first move has been made. And yet—could that be Tamara? Could that flat bosom ever have contained a singer's lungs? Could those mild eyes . . . ? He shook his head. Surely one could not change as much as that.

He followed her from the room. She was just vanishing round the corner. He hurried. She was sauntering with every appearance of unconcern, down the stairs. Suddenly she gave an exclamation of dismay. She broke into an agitated run, tripping from stair to stair with the oddly gliding movement that he had noticed before.

She reached the hall and sped across it as if she were taking part in a race. Skirts rustling, jewels flashing, bracelets jangling, she vanished through a far door.

Kardos could see no reason for her sudden agitation. True a

young woman stood at the foot of the stairs but she was looking up at him, not after the fleeing woman.

"Good evening, Mr. Kardos," she said in a curiously flat voice. "I'm Miss Harkness."

Kardos was taken completely by surprise—not only by the contrast to the woman of his imagination but by her actual appearance. A slight look of revulsion passed over his face. That hair, those clothes, that face. So—so ungarnished. Like the calf's head straight from the butcher.

The next instant his thoughts were hidden. He smiled, showing a fine set of his own strong white teeth. His expression registered amusement, admiration and astonishment, nicely blended. "You are Miss Harkness? And there was I expecting the elderly lady with the suspicious look." He laughed heartily.

"But should I be suspicious?" Sara asked coolly. His momentary recoil had not been lost on her.

Kardos was not to be discomposed a second time. "In my young days I spent my life travelling—from place to place, from country to country. And always I find the suspicious landlady."

"I see." Sara smiled politely. "I was left this place some years ago and, for various reasons, I kept it on."

Kardos wagged an admiring head. "I have no complaint. It will be an added pleasure to have a young and pleasing padrona."

"Nothing very glamorous about me at the moment. I've been in the kitchen all the evening."

"But why should we not have the cold meal, eh? Or out of the tins. They are very good and very varied."

"The fuddy-duddies wouldn't like it. They get upset when anything is changed."

"The fudd—what was that word? I do not know him."

"It's just my brother's name for the old people who live here. You must forget it."

"It is forgotten already." Kardos added regretfully, "Indeed, I never really heard it, which was a pity, for it sounded good. But those old ladies, tell me? Are they *formidable?*"

"Not really. It's just their age."

"I found one of them in my room."

Sara's heart sank. "Miss Millamont. I am sorry. She is so inquisitive. They're all like that. The trouble is that they have nothing to occupy their minds."

"I understand. Do not give it a second thought. Perhaps I am lucky." His sombre tone belied his words. "I am a Hungarian. I have much to think of and to work for. It makes for elasticity."

"One of the old ladies is a Hungarian, Madame Kosetti." Sara's heart warmed a little towards him as it was meant to do. "She nearly went mad during the rising. You see—she's not very active. She couldn't do anything to help."

Kardos nodded. "I was luckier. I managed to get into Budapest—twice." It was true. He had had some old scores to settle. It had seemed an excellent opportunity.

Sara's heart softened still further. "That was very brave."

Kardos pulled a droll face. "With my figure one cannot hope to be the knight in shining armour. But this Madame Kosetti, I will meet with her?"

"Oh yes." Sara looked at him doubtfully. "She is rather temperamental and inclined to raise the roof."

Kardos nodded his head. "I too am temperamental. No doubt we raise the roof together, yes?"

He seemed to find the idea amusing. He continued to look amused, to chuckle, his mouth open so that she could see the gold fillings in his teeth. "And what big teeth you have, Grandma?" The absurd quotation slid into her mind unsought.

She said hurriedly, "I mustn't keep you any longer. The dining room is over there. Daisy will show you to your table."

"You are very kind." He held out his hand. She placed hers on it, feeling it close, warm and hard on her own.

She knew then that it was not dislike that she felt for this smiling rotund little man but fear. For some strange and undefined reason she was afraid of him.

She watched him cross the hall. So well groomed, so prosperous looking that a whole host of bright lights seemed to spring up around him. An expensive carpet unroll beneath his feet. Soft music play in the distance and white coated waiters hurry to serve him.

Why had he come? What did he want with No. 9? Was Alan right? Was he a friend of Magda Brooks but, if so, why the secrecy? He had given other reasons for his visit.

Sara frowned. Come to think of it, no one's reactions had been exactly normal—not even her own.

Chapter 3

Kardos sat down at the small table to which the sour faced Daisy had directed him. He shook out his napkin and looked about him.

Miss Millamont sat at a table with two other people. A tall pallid man with pale eyes and a little old woman in a hand-knitted silk frock. Her features were sharp, her eyes dark and shining as prunes. Her hands, he saw, were small, plump and dimpled. Incredibly she wore on her head an old black felt hat like an inverted pudding basin.

Not much gets past that one, he thought, but she is not Tamara. Hair can be dyed but black eyes remain black eyes—and are not to be found with red hair.

His gaze moved on.

A second table was laid for one but unoccupied. At a third sat a mountain of a woman with marigold coloured hair and wearing a red velvet frock. With her was a mannish-looking female with crimped grey hair and a high colour. She sat in a wheel chair with a pair of crutches beside her.

Daisy put a plate in front of him and a round fire-proof dish piled high with Spaghetti Bolognaise. Kardos was pleasantly surprised. So the plain Miss Harkness does not immolate herself in vain, he thought, sprinkling cheese onto his plate.

Presently he had the feeling that he was being watched. He looked across the room. The woman in the wheel chair was staring at him with a look of surprising malignity. She did not avert her eyes when he turned his head but held him with the fierce blaze of her small eyes.

Kardos was startled. Could she be Tamara? And, if so, was this an open declaration of war? Or had the woman some other reason for her look? Did she perhaps dislike Hungarians—or men in general?

Mentally he shook his head. He could not believe that she was Tamara. The idea offended his every instinct. And yet would either of the others be more acceptable? That monstrous mound of flesh for instance? Could he once have been her lover? He shuddered inwardly at the thought.

He looked across again at the two women. The crippled one now had her head bent over her plate. The other, Madame Kosetti, he supposed, sat directly beneath an electric light bulb so that her great yellowish slab of a face was patched with light and shadow. Her immense coils of hair rose steeply above a fine brow. Her chins ran into the neck of her gown and her eyes were slow and vigilant and set in creases of fat.

She pushed her empty plate away from her with a gusty sigh of repletion. She sat back, staring at him inscrutably from beneath thick heavy lids.

Kardos' thoughts raced. Here was character. And fires not yet entirely burnt out. But was she Tamara Lubova? How could he know?

The dining room door opened. Magda Brooks came in. From the maid's welcoming, if wintry smile, it was plain that the newcomer was a favourite. Perhaps she too gives the tips, Kardos thought cynically. Magda saw Kardos. A look of astonishment passed over her face. The next moment it had gone, replaced by one of well-bred indifference. So she knows me, Kardos thought. She has seen me on television perhaps. Well, at least, she is too young to be Tamara.

He thought too that it would be pleasant to have an affair with her. With her smooth oval face, small perfect features, brilliant almost honey coloured eyes and trim plump figure, she should be capable of making even such an experienced lover as himself very happy.

His eye priced the black frock, the fur cape, the single row of well matched pearls. Her presence at No. 9, he judged, was as incongruous as his own.

Magda's thoughts too were busy. She alone in the house had a television set. A set strictly for her own enjoyment. She had made a point of seeing the programme in which Kardos had appeared; for she had long known and admired his voice, that rich lyric tenor of peculiar warmth and mellowness. And, because of her admiration she had taken the trouble to find out something of the man. His love affairs, his reputation for unscrupulous dealings, his implacability when he thought himself injured.

There were numerous stories about him. None of them reassuring nor endearing.

And now he was here, prosperous, suave, as unlikely looking as an orchid in a tomato house. Why? Had one of the old ladies, with their gift for intrigue, managed to fool him into thinking that the Lake of Fire was to be found here? If so, she trembled for her. Istvan Kardos was not the man to suffer such an indignity without taking his revenge.

And there was Sara. Sara, who at the first sign of trouble, would rally so staunchly, and probably so incompetently, to their defence.

Magda decided, with ironic detachment, that if she were going to interfere on the old ladies' behalf, she might as well include Sara in her benevolent schemes. And that young woman certainly needed someone to take her in hand.

Magda felt more cheerful than she had done for a long time, for she was naturally a managing woman. Or she had been up to three years ago.

A fruit salad of no particular merit or demerit followed the first course. Then everyone seemed on the move. Miss Millamont, with that odd little duck of the head that somehow continued to be both sentimental and sly. Her companion, now fully revealed in a tight-fitting frock with a drooping hem line, appearing to Kardos' fascinated gaze to have the appearance of a small ageing banana. The elderly man, his pale staring eyes resting on the newcomer unblinkingly as he passed, yet with apparent disinterest.

It was only later that Kardos decided to distrust that look. The most dangerous of cover men were like that, quiet, inconspicuous.

The two women at the other table left the room. The one large and muscular as a man. Madame Kosetti waddled past, breathing heavily. Kardos saw with fastidious disgust that she wore brocade bedroom slippers and that above them her ankles were swollen and discoloured.

As he left the room Magda spoke, introducing herself, "I can't be mistaken. It is Mr. Istvan Kardos, isn't it? I saw you on television a few weeks ago and for years before that I have been an admirer of yours. But what are you doing here?"

Kardos bowed. He smiled and his eyes showed his admiration. "My appearance here is due to my previous appearance on television. Ah, what a mistake! I enquire for Tamara Lubova, whom between ourselves I had practically forgotten, and I find dozens of Tamara Lubovas, or rather, they find me. Madame, think of the persecution. They ring me up. They call. They write. What shall I do? It is biological fact that, for glandular reasons, tenors tend to be short and excessively round, just as basses tend to be tall and thin. I am not then the romantic figure."

Magda laughed. "And you came here to escape? But how did you hear of it?"

"Through my doctor. I consult Dr. Gellibus. Go out of London, he says. I cannot afford it, I say. Try Seamarsh, he says, for he has relatives here. It is cheap and healthy—and there will be no Tamaras—or so he says."

"Gellibus? He must be related to the people who have the large furniture shop in the High Street." It stood on a prominent corner site. Magda wondered if Kardos had seen the name while on his way to No. 9. "But do sit down. I find yours such a fascinating predicament. And I'm very much afraid that your doctor friend is going to prove wrong."

"About what? Not Tamara?"

"Indeed, yes. There's Miss Millamont." Could it have been Miss Millamont who had written? "She has, I suspect, led a singularly uneventful life. In recompense she hints at all sorts of mysteries and intrigues in her life. That she is connected in some way with the Hapsburgs. Or, even more unlikely, that her income is derived from some mysterious source in Vienna. It is all quite fantastic and absurd."

"That is the lady with all the little gems?" His fingers flickered in a gesture that seemed to recreate them on his own person. "Her name certainly is not Austrian."

"Miss Millamont," said Magda in her positive way, "is the most English thing there is—a romantic and frustrated spinster."

Kardos laughed. "You think that she has never been to Austria? That it all comes from here?" He tapped his forehead.

"I think that she has lived in Vienna at some time in her life. She speaks of it with knowledge—so far as I can judge."

"You have been there perhaps?"

"Several times. It is a lovely city."

Kardos looked at her admiringly. "It is a city that would suit you very well. But what do you do here? Forgive me if I appear intrusive but it is plain that this is not your proper background."

Magda's face hardened a little. "My husband was a civil engineer. I lost him in South Africa where he was helping to build a dam. So I came here to be near my uncle, who is a solicitor, and somehow I've just stayed on."

Kardos looked sympathetic. "You have not the heart to make the new life? I think that very sad." He thought too that from her expression, Magda Brooks had not got on very well with her husband.

"I shall be moving on some day, I suppose." She picked up her handbag and rose to her feet. "And remember! You have been warned. As soon as someone tells Miss Millamont of your old love affair, she'll begin to think herself into the part of Tamara Lubova—and a singularly unstable and romantic one at that."

"She shall take no harm from me. I will be the soul of discretion."

"Thank you. She's a pathetic little thing." Magda lowered her voice, "Before we get to the lounge tell me, could you bear some rather bad bridge?"

"If you can," said Kardos, holding open the door for her, "I can." He foresaw that in Magda he was to have a useful source of information.

They left the dining room together. They were both very pleased with each other. As pleased as two people can be who each believe that they have deceived the other.

Sara went down the passage to the sitting room which was also the office. She went in and closed the door.

A large looking glass was fastened to the wall to create the illusion of light. She had glanced into it a dozen times a day without paying much attention to what she saw. Now she switched on all the lighting and walked up to it. Staring into it, a little frown of concentration on her forehead.

She saw an untidy looking young woman who appeared more than her age. Pale hair parted in the centre and dragged carelessly back into a bun. A long bony face, hollow cheeked and sharply angled. A fine skin, rough and burnt by the stove and entirely without make-up. A broad forehead, grey eyes surrounded by short stubby but very thick pale lashes. A figure too thin for curves. A grey knitted jumper chosen originally for practicability and now washed out and shapeless. A tweed skirt that sagged at the back. Narrow feet in flat shoes which would have been the better for cleaning.

So that was what five years in Seamarsh had done to her. No wonder that well dressed and comfortable people like Mr. Kardos looked at her with amazement. Recoiled involuntarily as from something repugnant.

She went on staring but now she no longer saw her reflection. She saw instead the passing years.

She recalled how her heart had dropped when she had first seen No. 9, large, grey, hideously ornate and yet somehow bleak and forbidding. It was a feeling that had changed to panic as the heavy front door had swung to behind her. She had felt stifled, imprisoned. The hall, with its tessellated floor, its shrouding stained glass windows, its pot plants in every shade of green, its passages winding weirdly away into a faint, shadowy and unknown distance, all spoke of another age, of a different order. In a moment of vision she had seen herself as inheriting the full burden of its past.

Then Alan had slipped his arm through hers, roaring with laughter at what had so frightened her. The moment of truth had passed, only to be revived now, five years later. Five years, during which No. 9, like a voracious monster, had swallowed up the girl that she had been.

Not that it had been all work. She and Alan had gone to dances, to parties, to first nights. He had seemed to like to take her out. No, he *had* liked it, and no one could have been gayer or a better companion. It was only during the last two years that things had changed. The parties were still there but only Alan went to them. She had been too tired, too shabby. She frowned thoughtfully. Or had it been that Alan had stopped asking her to go out with him?

She recalled the warnings, the hints that had been dropped by old friends—before they had disappeared from the scene. Been superseded by older, more successful men and women. She had turned a deaf ear to their warnings. Had scarcely noticed when they had ceased to come to No. 9. Had accepted Alan's careless explanation that old so-and-so had become a bore, a mischief maker, a dipsomaniac. She had gone on paying his debts, getting him out of scrapes, taking his side, right or wrong. And for what?

She was back again full circle to Mr. Kardos and his instinctive movement of revulsion.

The door opened. Alan came in. Stepped into the brittle and unreal looking-glass world.

"Any coffee going?"

"Daisy will be bringing it soon." She examined him curiously in the glass. How elegant he looked—and how handsome. Almost beautiful but for once, his appearance left her unmoved.

Alan threw himself into the one comfortable chair. "And what might you be doing?"

"I was thinking of how I'd let myself go."

"You certainly don't do a fellow much credit." He looked at her fleetingly. Then down at his hands, clasped between his knees. "But that's mostly my fault, isn't it? I mean—I haven't been pulling my weight. And—and—well, I seem to have been making a muck of most things lately."

"They certainly haven't gone too well," said Sara in a hard voice.

"I know. But I've been thinking."

"So have I."

"Yes but you haven't to reproach yourself—except for keeping a sponger like me about the place." Alan frowned painfully. "It isn't just that I don't want you to sell the house. It's realising suddenly that someone has the power to put you out." He hesitated. Then he said humbly, "Sara, let's start again. Let me take on the boiler and the fuddy-duddies just to show I'm willing."

Sara stared at his reflection, scepticism on her own face. "You know you'd never be up to see to the boiler."

"I thought that I could make it up later at night, since I go to bed later than you do. Then it wouldn't want making up as early."

"I suppose it wouldn't."

Alan looked hurt. "At least we could give it a trial."

"Yes, why not?" At the worst it would mean a few days' respite. A little longer in bed in the morning. "If you took on the boiler it'd be a tremendous help."

"No, it's the fuddy-duddies as well. All or nothing. Take it or leave it." He smiled anxiously at her.

"I'll take it," she said as the maid came in with the coffee. "Everything all right, Daisy?"

"Yes, miss. And they'd be glad if Mr. Alan could make up a fourth at bridge."

"Right. I'll go up. At least I'll have my coffee and go." He grinned at his sister. "Reformed from now on. That's me."

She nodded. He'd better be. She was surprised at her own harshness. "And Mr. Kardos?" She poured out a cup of coffee for herself and one for Alan.

"He's settling down all right, miss. He enjoyed his dinner." Daisy added, "Mrs. Brooks spoke to him and asked him to play bridge."

Sara looked up quickly. "D'you think she knew him before?"

"Before he came here? Oh no, miss. She recognised him after seeing him on the telly. Always been an admirer of his, she told him. Although what she meant by it I couldn't say."

"She probably meant that she admired his singing."

"Then he is the singer," said Alan slowly.

"It looks like it—although I can't imagine what made him come here."

"He's an evil man," Daisy declared. "Making up to that Mrs. Brooks—and her a rich widow. Mark my words, miss, nothing but ill will come from his being in this house."

"Daisy, you mustn't say things like that. It's bad for business."

The angular maidservant closed her eyes. "To one is given by the Spirit the word of wisdom; to another prophecy." She picked up the tray and stalked from the room.

"Wonder which that was?" Alan chuckled. "Poor old Daisy! It's almost time for her yearly jamboree. She always gets a bit queer round about now."

"There're several anniversaries coming round besides the Convocation of the Watchful People," said Sara gloomily. "The death of old Mrs. Harkness for one. And if Daisy's going to prepare for the end of the world again it'll be the last straw. Denouncing people. Slipping out to pray in that extraordinary chapel of hers just when I want her most."

Alan looked hurt. "You don't expect me to be of much help, do you?"

"You know that no one could take Daisy's place. But if she's going to get religious mania Mr. Kardos is just the sort to have her up for defamation of character." Sara broke off, sighing in exasperation. "Oh, why did he have to come here?"

"Yes, that is rather a question, isn't it? What reason did he give in his letter?"

"That he'd been recommended to come to Seamarsh by his doctor. That the Town Council had given him this address. That the terms attracted him.

"There you are then. Three perfectly good reasons."

"The third reason he gave makes nonsense of the others. He looks worth a million. He even smells like it."

"He might be temporarily embarrassed. That could mean anything from a bookmaker to income tax. What does he look like?"

"Like a foreigner. Very anxious to shake hands. He smiles

a lot, too. But, for all that, there's something faintly sinister about him. His eyes are—sort of watchful. And his mouth shuts in a straight line.''

"The gangster type, eh? Now, who have we got worth robbing? There's only the fair Magda."

Said Sara slowly, "I was wondering about that. Wondering whether he had come here to see her. They may only have pretended not to know each other to stop the old ladies talking.''

"You think he really might be courting her? But he's an old man.''

"I don't suppose he thinks so." Sara shrugged. "He'll soon have enough of the place and its eccentricities. He's already caught Miss Millamont in his bedroom.''

"What?" Alan stared. "Oh Lor'! Then tomorrow you'll have him complaining that his studs have gone or some other trumpery thing. Yes, you're too right. He'll be going.''

"I don't believe Miss Millamont does steal.''

"Well dear, that shows a very nice spirit. But you know jolly well we're always having complaints. And Daisy herself saw her taking the last of the crackers off the Christmas tree and stuffing them up her jumper.''

"I don't believe it. Besides, whatever would she have wanted with crackers?''

"Miss Millamont always has her screwy reasons. Probably she and Mrs. McGee had a midnight feast in one of the bedrooms and pulled them then. You know how Mrs. McGee is always lamenting the lovely lost days of her innocent childhood and Miss Millamont listens fascinated. But *simply fascinated.*''

"And I suppose tomorrow she'll be wearing Mr. Kardos' studs among all her bits and pieces?" Sara sighed, she put down her empty cup. "I'm going out for the bread now. I only hope Dunn is at home. If not I'll have to go again tomorrow before breakfast.''

"If anyone goes out before breakfast it'll be me," said Alan. Adding with an anxious glance, "Only you'll have to call me. You know how I sleep.''

"I'll do that." Sara's smile was faintly derisive. "Never mind, perhaps it won't happen. Dunn may be there this evening.''

"I hope so." Alan grinned. "I'm not all that reformed." He put his hands on her shoulders and said seriously, "I'll get myself a job—and stick to it. You'll see.''

When Sara had left the room he strolled over to the looking glass. He approved of what he saw there. The straight, slim figure, the smooth cap of gold, the fine features, the brilliant blue eyes.

He smiled experimentally and remarked to his reflection, "The return of the prodigal. A very moving performance—if I say it myself."

Sara went briskly along the flagged passage and into the hall. She took her coat from a cupboard. She pulled a silk square out of its pocket and tied it over her hair.

She turned towards the front door, then paused, frowning a little.

There was nothing to hear. Nothing out of the ordinary to see. Yet as she stood in the poorly lighted hall she was aware of some intangible change. Like a prison warder or an attendant in a mental home she had become sensitive to atmosphere. Grown to know instinctively when something was wrong.

The elderly man, who sat at Miss Millamont's table, came out of the lounge, a copy of the *Telegraph* in his hand.

"Thought I heard someone. What are you doing, Sara, eh? Going out? At this time?"

"We've run out of bread."

Sara wondered what he thought about. And which was the real Mr. Gadsby? The negative, inoffensive figure who seemed to ask questions more from habit than from any real curiosity? Or that other Mr. Gadsby whom she had once surprised?

She opened the front door and let herself out, breathing in the fresh cold air thankfully as she hurried along.

When she got back with the bread Magda was standing in the hall, idly turning the pages of a fashion magazine. Her mink cape was draped carelessly over one shoulder. She held a cigarette in her hand. She looked in that Victorian setting oddly out of place, as if she had slipped back in time.

She looked up. "It's you, Sara." Her tone was unaccountably friendly. "I'm dummy so I just stepped out for a smoke. Mr. Gadsby is such a slow player it gets on my nerves."

"I've been out for some bread," said Sara briefly.

"Must you work so hard? You sound sometimes like an old woman." She added with cruel emphasis, "A *dull* old woman. It's stupid at your age."

"It's the house. And the fuddy-duddies. They are a bit much."

"It's not the house. Nor the fuddy-duddies and you know it. It's . . ." Magda broke off to nod to Kardos whom she saw standing just outside the lounge door, partly obscured by a bead curtain.

Alan, Sara thought. That's what she was going to say. Everyone had been saying it for years only I wouldn't listen.

Kardos stepped forward. The bead curtain jingled slightly. The shadows moved in bewildering array and his footsteps made a slight slapping sound like fish on a marble slab.

"I interrupt the gossip, yes?" He divided a gold-tooth smile between them.

"Only a little one." Magda reacted to men instinctively. Her smile was a charming one if a little absent-minded. She turned back to Sara. "It's Alan who's the trouble, of course. But even with him round your neck need you be quite such a dreary?" Magda held the opinion, shared by a good many English people, that foreigners, however long resident in the country, still could not understand what was said to others in front of them.

"You're too damned serious, Sara," she went on. "You should snap out of it." Then she added surprisingly, "That slightly gaunt look of yours is pretty distinguished really. It wants dressing up to. It's a pity we aren't the same size. Then I could have lent you something decent to wear. We might still manage a hat—or furs, and I could do something with your hair."

Sara stared in amazement, fascinated too by the mental picture of herself with one of Magda's bits of nonsense on her plain head. Wearing the mink coat. Or perhaps the ocelot would suit her better? The whole idea seemed so absurd that she laughed aloud and the colour ran up under her pale skin.

She's right, Kardos thought. This Miss Harkness might be distinguished, not beautiful, but that rare thing, distinguished. But it would not happen. She had not the will.

Suddenly from upstairs came a burst of glorious sound. It was the aria "Che gelida manina."

"That is me—my voice." Kardos' agitation was obvious. Was this signal to himself from Tamara? He was in the mood to see signs and portents everywhere.

"It must be Madame Kosetti's gramophone," said Sara. "She has a large collection of records."

"I have never heard her playing that one before," said Magda.

"Then it must be meant as a compliment to Mr. Kardos,"

said Sara. How tiresome everyone was being. She tried to keep a note of impatience out of her voice.

Alan came from the lounge. "Are you two coming to finish the rubber?" he asked. "Old man Gadsby is getting a bit restive." He looked radiant, full of animation and good humour. "I suppose that caterwauling is coming from Madame Kosetti's room. She must have the door open."

Magda turned on him fiercely. "Alan, you beastly Philistine; it's not caterwauling. It's a wonderful song, wonderfully sung."

Alan looked at her insolently. He shrugged. "Have it your own way." Adding carelessly, "Wonder how long it'll go on? Until one or other of the old ladies rushes in and protests I suppose. Then there'll be arguments, screams and finally hysterics."

The song came to an end. Nothing followed but silence. A silence in which the echoes of sound seemed for a time to linger and all four of them stood listening attentively.

"No more?" said Alan. "That's rummy."

"When the voice goes it is as if a golden star falls," said Kardos heavily.

Later, alone in his bedroom, he pulled a chair into the area of warmth engendered by the electric fire. He sat down thinking over the events of the evening.

Had that song been a message from Tamara? Or had it been, as that so strangely beautiful young man had said, merely caterwauling coming from Madame Kosetti's room?

Caterwauling! What an expression to use. The English were, after all, a race of barbarians, fit only for those wars which, despite all their protestations of being peace-loving, they waged with such frequency, gusto and endurance.

The gramophone was playing again. The sound came to him softly. Music from operas it was true but none that seemed to have special significance.

The music ceased abruptly in the middle of the overture to "Traviata." Had Mrs. McGee trundled into the other woman's bedroom and turned it off? Were they up there now, quarrelling, hissing like geese at each other across the now silent gramophone?

He became aware that he was sitting tense, strung up, in a state of expectancy. But if he were expecting some further move from Tamara obviously he was to be disappointed. The hands of his watch showed him that an hour had passed and she had not come.

Did she then mean him to go to look for her?

He half rose. Then he sank down again. If he were to go to a bedroom its occupant had only to scream and accuse him of forcing his way in to have him turned out of the house.

He grinned to himself unpleasantly. He was too old a hunter to be caught like that.

His thoughts ran on, began to make a coherent pattern.

He had made the address of Tamara Lubova come to him: why should he not do the same for her identity? Could he not short-circuit his search for her by enlisting the help of Miss Harkness? She was a young woman ripe for sympathy. Caught up in a drab environment in which any colour and romance would surely appeal to her.

But how to arouse her sympathies?

Presently Kardos nodded his head, slowly and with conviction. That was it. If Tamara had made no move by—say lunch time next day, he would go to Miss Harkness. Tell her of the broadcast. Of the arrival of the totally unexpected letter. Of his remorse at ever having brought up Tamara's name. Of his fears that, in some way, he might have brought her into danger.

Yes, that was good—as far as it went. But he must have some evidence to back up his story. Then he had it.

The envelope in which the letter had come! He would say that someone had steamed it open before it had reached him. Someone who would have no difficulty in tracing its place of origin. Someone who had had twenty-four hours' start . . .

In the silence and emptiness of his room he laughed aloud. It was a good story. And how lucky that he had slit the envelope along the top with a paper knife instead of tearing it open. Now he had only to steam the flap, stick it down again. . . .

He took it from his notecase. Turned it over in the light. His smile faded. A vein throbbed at his temples and his eyes grew venomous. It was true. What he had thought of as a figment of his imagination was a fact.

Someone *had* steamed the letter open and then resealed it.

Chapter 4

The next day was dull and blustery with wind. A steely sky pressed down on the melancholy of the decaying Square and all the houses were filled with a sad grey light.

Sara's spirits were unaffected. She was humming cheerfully to herself as she rummaged in a cupboard. The forebodings of last night had gone.

She came on what she wanted. A once expensive green and black Italian sweater and narrow black stretch pants. She put them on and looked at herself appraisingly in the glass.

"That slightly gaunt look of yours is pretty distinguished really!" Gaunt? Distinguished? It wasn't exactly what one wanted to be but perhaps it was the best one could do at twenty-seven. And she certainly had an elegant figure, slim, long and flat. The make-up was an improvement too.

She decided, as she ran downstairs, that she would reorganise the work so as to give herself more free time. Furthermore she would insist that the old ladies conform to a more conventional way of life. And that, in future, Alan should get out of his own scrapes and pay his own debts.

The lunatic optimism of this did not dishearten her. She would, she told herself, present Mr. Carron when next they met with a complete blue print for the future.

Mr. Gadsby, she saw, was reading a newspaper on his favourite seat among the potted plants in the centre of the hall. Mrs. McGee and Miss Millamont were in earnest conversation in a far corner. Sara wondered what they could be talking about. Mrs. McGee usually thought Miss Millamont too stupid to bother about.

Alan was in the office reading the morning's newspaper. He looked at her with a quizzical interest. "So the sacrifice of my valuable time is not to be in vain," he commented. "We must follow this up and go out somewhere this evening. What shall it be? London? Old friends? Or just the local?''

''Let's go to the local.'' She unlocked a drawer of her desk and took out her account books.

Daisy came into the room to collect the used breakfast things. ''That Miss Millamont's at it again,'' she said. Her narrow face expressed her disapproval of her young mistress's changed appearance. ''Declared that someone had searched her room during the night and that there St. Nicholas had gone from her mantelpiece. The new gentleman was very concerned. All over her he was. Then Mrs. Brooks said she supposed that some emissary of the Hapsburgs had taken the statuette and that seemed to damp down his interest.''

''But it won't damp down our Miss Millamont,'' Alan remarked. ''She'll go on making a fuss until she gets tired of it. Then St. Nicholas will reappear and we shall have peace—until the next time.''

Sara reflected that this was one of the eccentricities she had meant to forbid in the future. ''Miss Millamont,'' she had planned to say, ''one more imaginary burglar and you'll have to leave.''— But she had not had time to say it. Now she had a sneaking suspicion that she never would.

''You'll never stop it,'' said Alan, almost as if he had read her thoughts. ''Anything said to Miss Millamont goes in one ear and out the other without making any impression en route.''

Daisy clattered the things on the tray. ''There're worse things than Miss Millamont's crazy notions. That Mr. Kardos for one, with his voice like soft soap and his eyes like brown windsor soup—only not as wholesome.'' She added severely to Sara, ''And, if you ask me, miss, this is no time to be dressing yourself up and painting your face.'' She went away, muttering to herself.

''Almost as if I were Jezebel,'' said Sara, with a weak giggle. ''Still, it is aggravating of Miss Millamont.''

''She's not the only one. Madame Kosetti's ill in bed again. She gave several realistic groans when I took up her breakfast tray but actually I thought she looked jolly well.'' That was another thing Sara had meant to stop, Madame Kosetti's rest cures.

The four old ladies lived under the roof. A warren of a place with rooms here and there, odd shaped windows and skylights, inconsequent steps, unexpected corners and a door which opened onto the roof. Originally they had been on the floor below but this had necessitated their moving in the height of the season. Sara had been adamant about this.

In the face of their complaints, their cries of protest and indignation, of Madame Kosetti's hysterics and Mrs. Bradshaw's indignant asides to her deceased husband, Sara had remained unmoved. She must be free to let all the rooms possible in the summer if she were to keep the place running during the winter.

The old ladies had fought a fierce but losing rearguard action, metaphorically defending every stair of the last flight that led to the attics. Once there, however, the charm of being completely on their own had appealed to them. The amount of space had delighted them.

With the heartless greed of the very old they had plundered the rooms left empty by the death of two of their number. Mrs. Winfield's paste studded handglass had been translated into Miss Millamont's mysterious and romantic past. Her fur-lined slippers had become part of Mrs. McGee's wardrobe. Her mattress helped to support Madame Kosetti's mountainous weight. Her flight of plaster swallows now flew across Mrs. Bradshaw's walls.

The late Madame Rakosi's collection of foreign romantic novels had been the cause of a fierce internecine warfare, now appearing in one room, now in another, until Miss Millamont had hidden them under the floorboards in her room, since when they had been practically destroyed by mice.

Only Mr. Gadsby, compliant as ever, still moved from one floor to the next, according to the seasons.

There was a timid knock on the door. Miss Millamont fluttered in. She took a seat on the very edge of her chair and stared at Sara with apprehensive eyes. She looked so small, so forlorn and defeated that Sara felt her exasperation turn to pity. If Miss Millamont's behaviour upset other people, she reflected, it seemed to upset Miss Millamont even more.

"Daisy tells me that you've lost your St. Nicholas," she remarked. "We must see what we can do to find it."

Miss Millamont shook her head so vigorously that all the stiff little curls danced on her head. "I don't want anyone to do anything," she said with a fluttering gesture of her hands.

Sara stared. Usually the least that would satisfy Miss Millamont was a thorough search of the house and a notice put up in the hall. "Has the statue been returned then?"

"No—not yet. But I don't really mind. I mean—if he has taken it, then let him keep it."

"Who do you mean by him?" Sara asked curiously. Alan?

Mr. Gadsby? Or some dark unidentified stranger? Miss Millamont had a fertile imagination.

The question threw Miss Millamont into a flutter. "No one. No one at all. Just a figure of speech. The truth is—I didn't really lose the figure. At least—I'd grown tired of it." Miss Millamont was floundering under Sara's astonished gaze. She drew a deep breath and added, in the rather smug tone of one producing at last a perfectly rational explanation, "Mrs. McGee said that to keep it was a Popish practice. And there's the Second Commandment too." And then weakening, "Though I did think St. Nicholas *rather* sweet." Her soft lips quivered. But she pressed them firmly together and sat up very straight and resolute looking in her chair.

"But that's nonsense, Miss Millamont. Your St. Nicholas was fascinating and no one could object to him. Of course, you must have him back."

"But I don't want him back. I only want the whole thing forgotten." Miss Millamont was upset again. She sat locking and unlocking her fingers and her small head shook with agitation like a faded flower stalk in an open field. "No, I've quite decided. I intend to turn over a new leaf. No more romantic stories. No more embroidering of facts. Just the plain unvarnished truth from now on."

She looked so depressed at this that Sara cast round in her mind for something to say to cheer her up. She remarked kindly, "The truth about your life may seem dull to you but I expect it would seem very interesting and exciting to other people."

Miss Millamont sighed heavily. "It was dull. Very dull. For instance, did you know that my father was vicar of Little Bodmin?"

Sara stared. "The village near here?"

Miss Millamont nodded. "I'd known your cousin, Mr. Harkness, and Mr. Carron since childhood. That's how I came to make my home here after my return from Austria."

"You'd been living abroad? That must have been very interesting and romantic."

Miss Millamont shook more than ever. "It was nothing of the sort. I was governess to the children of an Austrian banker—and nothing can be duller than that. A governess has no status. No status at all. She exists in a vacuum. She is neither one of the family nor one of the servants." She gave a small tinkling laugh. "I can assure you that nothing can be more humdrum than being a governess. Of course, there was a great deal of entertaining.

Mrs. Foeldi was a very beautiful woman, very gay and viva-
cious. And her husband was devoted to her and a very wealthy
man. There was always something going on but I was in the
schoolroom and scarcely saw my employers. Later, after the
war, it was different.''

"You were there during the war?'' Miss Millamont's latest
story, true or not, was beguiling Sara against her will.

"Oh, yes. The *first* war, of course. Such a terrible time.
Austria was ruined. In a state of revolution. The Foeldis lost
everything. They had difficulty even in keeping from starving.
We were living on the top floor of a tenement at the time. Just
the five of us, Mr. and Mrs. Foeldi, the two children, Andras
and Marietta, and myself. Papa was still alive then. He wanted
me to come home but how could I leave them? They needed me
and little Andras had always been so delicate.

"But it was a terrible place. You can have no idea.'' Miss
Millamont wriggled more comfortably into her chair. "Whole
families living in one room—and not only families but people
who'd come together for no good purpose. Thieves, robbers and
worse. And women—who, I fear, were not very respectable.
The stairs were always dark and slippery with rotting vegetable
leaves. The banister had gone in places so that one had to keep
close to the inner wall. Not too close, of course, because of the
damp and the queer patches of green slime. It was the damp that
killed Andras. He was only ten and such a handsome, affection-
ate little fellow. He died in the second autumn after the war. Of
course, we'd lost Marietta before that—and the double blow
killed their mother. Her heart was broken and she had lost all
desire to go on living.''

"What happened to Marietta? Did she die too?''

"We never knew what happened to her,'' Miss Millamont's
voice was abstracted. She seemed to have lost herself in the old
sad days of defeat. She had stopped shaking and her voice was
firmer. "I suppose we'd grown careless. After all, we'd been
there eighteen months and nothing had happened. Perhaps we
forgot that Marietta was growing up. She was just fifteen and
promised to be as lovely as her mother. Her hair was like a flame
and her eyes such a marvellous blue. Not cold eyes like Alan's,
but warm, soft.''

"But what had happened to her?'' Sara wished people
would leave Alan alone.

"She went out early one morning and never came back.
Mrs. Foeldi couldn't leave Andras but Mr. Foeldi and I searched

all day. We called on shops and friends. We went to the police and they searched the tenement but it was no use. Marietta had disappeared as completely as if the ground had opened and swallowed her up. For weeks afterwards, whenever we heard a woman scream either I or Mr. Foeldi, if he were in, would go downstairs to investigate but it was never Marietta. Once, I remember, I met some men carrying a body out after dark. I made them uncover it. It *was* a young girl but it was not Marietta." Miss Millamont added simply, "It was after that that I began to pray that she was dead."

"And then what happened?"

"Gradually Mr. Foeldi's financial position improved. He got back some of his property and bought a small villa on the outskirts of Vienna but, poor man, by then his mind had given way and he had come to believe that Marietta had only gone on a visit and might be expected to return at any moment. When he died, just before the last war, he left me a small annuity and I came back to England."

Sara was silent a moment. "Weren't you ever frightened? Looking for poor Marietta in that tenement I mean?"

"Always," said Miss Millamont simply. "Sometimes my knees would shake so much afterwards that I could scarcely get upstairs."

Sara nodded. In her imagination she was in that overcrowded tenement where women screamed and corpses were smuggled out at night. Said she slowly, "Don't you see, Miss Millamont, the true account of your life is much more romantic and mysterious than anything you made up. Why," she added, still pondering the story, "it makes you quite a different sort of person."

Miss Millamont returned abruptly to the present. The tenderness and remembered grief drained from her face. Her glance sharpened, grew almost hostile. "It does nothing of the sort. I'm just a harmless old woman. A poor clergyman's daughter. Someone who has spent her whole life as a governess." She leaned forward and clawed at Sara's arm. "That's what I want you to remember. That and nothing more. That's what I want everyone to know. You must tell them that. Not the other." She spoke with rising excitement and her faded eyes were frightened. "Nothing about being mysterious or brave. Promise you will. Promise."

Sara considered the scared blue eyes, the trembling clutching hand. What on earth was Miss Millamont up to now? "Don't get so upset," she said soothingly. "If you want me to tell people that you were a parson's daughter and earned your living as a governess of course I will. Only—what people?''

"Everyone in the house. Just bring it up some time today. Only don't mention any details. Not even Austria."

"I think I'd have to do that." Sara spoke in a purposely matter of fact tone. "You see, everyone knows that you've lived in Vienna."

"Do they?" Miss Millamont's scared blue eyes went past Sara. Staring now here, now there. "Yes," she admitted at last, reluctantly. "I suppose you'll have to admit to that. But mind," her voice sank to a sibilant whisper, "nothing more. Nothing at all."

She rose to her feet, fluttering with a jingling of bangles to the door. She halted abruptly, as if something were written there. "Tell Mr. Kardos," she said without turning. "Especially Mr. Kardos."

She opened the door a very little way. She slipped through with an absurdly conspiratorial air and in spite of her size with some difficulty.

Sara was left staring at the closed door. Had she just heard the truth? Or had Miss Millamont set out on the screwiest, the most far-fetched of all her impersonations?

Istvan Kardos was not displeased with his progress. Already he knew a great deal about No. 9 and its inhabitants. During the small hours when everyone else had been asleep, he had explored the house. Then, that morning he had taken coffee with the widow, Magda Brooks, in her comfortable suite. In a room so like others he knew in London, soft colours, the latest books from Harrods, stiffly arranged greenhouse flowers. He had plied Daisy with seemingly idle questions, ignoring her sullen reluctance, as she did his bedroom. He had penetrated to the top floor and introduced himself to Madame Kosetti as a fellow citizen of the now defunct Austro-Hungarian empire.

This last had been a meeting very much to his taste. True he had seen many such rooms. Those who had so little must conserve what they had. Curtains must be kept drawn to hide as far as possible the poverty of the land. Clothes must be worn until mouse, moth or age ravaged them beyond repair. Newspaper, in sufficient quantities, could be sold for a few shillings. All this was familiar. It was Madame Kosetti herself who gave to his visit its peculiar interest.

She had admitted to a great admiration for his singing, "so

exquisite in mezzo voce." She not only had the recording he had heard the previous evening but also his rendering of "Cielo e mar" from Ponchielli's "Gioconda" and that great tenor aria "O paradiso" from Meyerbeer's "L'Africana." An aria, she had said, embedded like a jewel in an otherwise worthless ragbag of odds and ends.

It was this sentence that remained in his mind. A jewel? Was she mocking him? Hinting at a parallel between the song, the Lake of Fire and her own circumstances? It was an interesting speculation.

After lunch he had sought out Miss Harkness and there everything had gone wrong.

She had listened to his story at first with bewilderment, then with a frank scepticism, wounding to his self-esteem. She had intimated that, in her view, he, Istvan Kardos, had been tricked, misled and by that poor creature, Miss Millamont.

"I don't see that your girl friend could possibly be here," she told him briskly. She looked amused. "Madame Kosetti is the only foreigner. She always speaks as if she were very well connected. And, although I can't go back as far as 1914, she does seem to know an awful lot about foreign nobility. You know! Who their mothers were and how she danced with their grandfathers at some ball or other when she was seventeen. All that sort of thing."

Kardos had met this with his own brand of cunning. "But how much do you really know of your guests?" He added with a great show of drollery, "Come, you English are said never to refuse a bet. I will bet you that you cannot tell me one solid fact about the past of each one of your boarders. What d'you say?"

"That you would lose." Sara paused to pick her facts. And in the silence that ensued became aware of the weight of his expectation coming towards her like a wave, pressing in on her. For some extraordinary reason her answer was really important to him.

"D'you know," she said easily, "I believe you'd win your bet after all. I took on the fuddy-duddies too late in their lives. What went on before then I just don't know."

If Kardos were disappointed he hid it well. He laughed merrily. "So I win the bet, yes? The bet that, unfortunately for me, was never actually made." He became serious. "But to return to this letter. . . ."

"I can't help feeling that you've been misled. I can see that the letter was typed on our paper, with our typewriter. It's an old one and its idiosyncrasies are unmistakable. But I still think it's a hoax. Not a deliberate one," Sara smiled. "But—well, there is Miss Millamont. She's incurably romantic and a bit mental. It's just the sort of thing I'd expect her to do. Particularly forgetting the diamond and having to steam open the letter so that she could add a postscript about it."

"But you have not the television for her to have seen the programme."

"Oh, that's easy. There's an old people's home which has a television set. Miss Millamont often slips in there after supper to watch. She thinks no one knows." Sara added, remembering Miss Millamont's injunction, "Not that she could possibly be Tamara Whats-it. Her father was vicar of Little Bodmin, a village quite near here."

Tamara Whats-it! The condescension! Kardos could willingly have struck the pale, composed face. The conversation was not going at all as he had planned. Miss Harkness was not a romantic. She was not looking for colour, sympathy and romance. On the contrary she would not recognise them if they came her way. She was typically English. Insensitive, arrogant, cold and unimaginative. And, he thought spitefully, so plain, with the long face of the horse.

Sara was speaking again. "Yes, the more I think of it the more certain I am that I'm right. Miss Millamont saw your programme. Identified herself with your [Kardos braced himself for a repetition of the offending nomenclature] ex-lady friend and typed you that letter." Adding as a happy afterthought, "That would account for her going into your room. All part of the romantic interlude she'd planned. She felt . . ."

Sara broke off suddenly. She had just seen the one fatal flaw in her reasoning.

Miss Millamont had *not* seen the television programme, "Out of the Past." Had known nothing of the Lake of Fire or its owner. Not, that is, until Mrs. McGee had enlightened her on the first floor landing that morning. And that was why she had ceased her play-acting. Had insisted that she, Sara, should tell Mr. Kardos her true history.

Sara, for a fleeting moment, wondered whether it was her true history. But true or not Miss Millamont had been actuated by fear. Fear of this plump rotund little man with his opaque brown eyes and gold-filled mouth . . .

She became aware that the said plump, rotund little man was watching her from across the other side of the desk. That there was something watchful, even menacing, in the leaden penetration of his gaze.

She attempted a smile. "What was I saying?"

Said Kardos, very softly and smiling too. "That Miss Millamont felt . . . something—but what?"

"Oh yes. Of course. I was going to say that Miss Millamont must have felt that she'd get to know you better like that. Know how to arouse your interest——" Sara hoped that she sounded convincing.

"But my interest has been aroused." The voice was almost purring. "Still, it would have been a little difficult for this Miss Millamont to know that Tamara Lubova had had red hair, would it not?"

"Not really." Now Sara was on firmer ground. "She was governess for years to a banker's family in Vienna. She could easily have heard of Tamara Whats-it. She may even have seen her and remembered the colour of her hair."

"Miss Harkness, you have an answer for everything."

"I'm pretty certain I'm right about this one." Sara thought suddenly how nice it would be if she could get rid of Mr. Kardos. "I tell you what I'll do. I'll cancel your booking and return you your money. What do you say?"

"I say, no." Kardos laid a muscular but well manicured hand on his breast. "I feel it in my heart. That letter is genuine. Somewhere here is my Tamara and I must find her." His words were soft but his eyes mocked her.

"Then you're going to stay your month?"

He shrugged. "My month—or longer. Until I am assured that my broadcast did no harm. On that one point, my dear Miss Harkness, we must differ. On that point but, I hope, on no other." Adding in a particularly suave voice, "And the name is Tamara Lubova."

He rose, flashed his gold teeth at her, bowed, turned on his heel and left the room, going so quietly that the closing of the door scarcely sounded.

Sara watched it, wide-eyed and incredulous. She seemed to be spending a lot of her time watching the closing of that particular door.

Her thoughts whirled. So Mr. Kardos really believed in the genuineness of that letter. He really thought that Madame Kosetti was his ex-girl friend, Tamara Lubova. (Something in the way the name had been thrown at her head had impressed it indelibly

on her mind.) And if he believed that, then he must believe that
the diamond too was somewhere in the house.

The more she thought of the idea the more unlikely it
appeared. True Madame Kosetti (And it must be Madame Kosetti.
She was the only foreigner in the house) kept her wardrobe
locked and wore the key round her neck night and day, but then
the old were secretive. Secretive and suspicious. It did not mean
that she had in her possession a diamond worth a fortune—and
nothing less would have interested the detestable Kardos.

Why, the old lady was always bewailing the fact that all her
valuables had been sold. She had enumerated them so often that
Sara sometimes fancied that she herself had actually seen them
go.

She looked about her at the shabby commonplace surroundings furnished with the cast-offs of other rooms. She could hear
the familiar clatter of crockery from the pantry opposite as Daisy
collected the afternoon tea things. A bold faced calendar, pre-
sented by the local dairy, gave the date, January 15th. The hands
of the clock on the mantelpiece were at half-past three. Everything combined to make nonsense of Istvan Kardos' story. He
must be mad. Quite mad.

But what could she do about it? That was the problem.
Should she warn Madame Kosetti? If so, in what words?

It was then that she thought of the two old ladies who had
died during the last two years. Could one of them have been
Tamara Lubova? There had been Mrs. Winfield, a wisp of a
woman, always cold, always complaining. And Madame Rakosi
who, even in old age, had retained the imprint of beauty. Aqui-
line features, flashing dark eyes, an imperious, if charming
manner.

Yes, Sara decided, Madame Rakosi and Tamara Lubova
might well have been one. If so, the collection of romantic
novels would not have been all that had been taken after her
death. There was the diamond, the Lake of Fire. And who had
that she, Sara, had no way of telling.

By this time she had involved herself in so many theories
and suppositions that she felt as if she were in the grip of a
particularly bewildering nightmare. One part of her brain accepted
her conclusions. The other repudiated them with weary scepticism.

What she wanted was not only a fresh mind to bear on the
subject but a trained mind. She recalled one friend who was
always ready to help her, Mr. Carron. Obviously he was the
person to consult.

She dialled the number of his office. He was in, the clerk told her, but he was engaged. Would she hold on for the moment, please.

She held on, elbow planted on the desk, her chin resting in the palm of her hand. She thought of Mr. Carron and at once felt better.

The firm of Harkness & Carron was an old established one, destined to end, at least under those names, with the passing of the remaining partner, Rupert Carron, now in his seventy-second year; for Mr. Harkness had left no children and Mr. Carron was a widower, who had lost his two sons in the last war. He was an urbane, alert old gentleman, his wits sharpened by half a century spent in listening to the follies and tragedies of his numerous clients.

It was very quiet in the room now. Daisy had gone from the pantry. The old wainscotting settled with a sudden crack. The door, moved by a momentary draught, came open. Shut again with a faint click, then opened.

The minutes passed. Sara was a little ashamed now of her panic, of what she began to think of as her gullibility. Mr. Carron would be amused. In fact it was going to be quite difficult to repeat to him Mr. Kardos' story—except perhaps on the grounds that she wanted to get rid of him. . . .

"Well, Sara? Sorry to have kept you waiting." The well bred old voice sounded suddenly in her ear. "What's the trouble? Nothing serious I hope."

"I don't think so. But it's a little difficult to explain." Sara hesitated, gulped. Then, "Do you ever watch a television programme called 'Out of the Past'?"

"I have done so at infrequent intervals." Mr. Carron held the old-fashioned but rather pleasant notion that women, on the whole, were charming, inconsequent creatures. Now it coloured the tone of his voice.

"Did you see one about three weeks ago? It was the life story of the Hungarian singer, Istvan Kardos?"

"No, I didn't see it. Should I have done so?"

"It would have made it easier for me to explain how he comes to be staying here."

"You have an opera singer staying at No. 9?" Sara could have kissed him for the amusement in his voice. "You are going up in the world." There was a pause. And then, in quite a different tone of voice, he said, "A Hungarian, eh?"

"Yes, a round, brown little man." Sara plunged into the

story that Kardos had told her. It sounded just as unlikely as it had at first. At every point she expected some expression of mirth or disbelief. Instead, except for a sudden intake of breath at the first mention of Tamara Lubova by name, there came only silence from the other end of the line. A silence that, for some reason, gradually formed a zone of unreality, strange, forbidding, enclosing the two of them and some far off echoes too faint to catch.

When she had finished Mr. Carron said briskly, "I think I'd better come round and see you. Then we can decide what is best to be done."

"But there isn't any truth in the story, is there?" Sara's voice had sharpened. "I mean—it is all nonsense, isn't it?"

"Sara my dear, don't sound so cross. It is true that the name Tamara Lubova has long been associated in my mind not only with romance but with No. 9. It is equally true that I never expected to hear it again. Your story of the diamond, I admit, comes as a complete surprise. However it does explain something that has long puzzled me. But don't worry, Sara. I'll come round right away. Let us leave matters until then."

The line went dead. Sara remained holding the receiver in her hand, her mind caught between incredulity and panic.

Then the story of Tamara was true. The thought brought with it a strange feeling of insecurity. A feeling that was to grow until it darkened her whole outlook.

It made strangers of the four old ladies. She saw their faces blank now and closed against her. She felt the chill of never having known them. And the house with its Edwardian furniture and stuffy hangings, was it too to become simply the sad symbol of someone else's past and she herself an interloper?

The door, clicking open, made her start. She had the uneasy notion that someone in the passage outside was pushing it open to see what she was doing.

She tried to dismiss the idea but it persisted. The narrow black crack and beyond it—what? or whom?

She sprang up and jerked the door open. The passage stretched emptily to right and left. Patterned by the dark shadows cast by ugly pieces of furniture and barred windows filled with opaque glass backed by ancient dust.

She heard her brother's light springy steps approaching down the back stairs. He made his graceful appearance. "I've almost run out of cigarettes. . . ." He broke off. "What's the matter with you?"

"I've been talking to Mr. Kardos."

A slightly wary look appeared on her brother's handsome face. "What did he have to say?"

"He was telling me about his television appearance—and how it had been followed by a letter written on our notepaper and our typewriter."

"Oh rot!" Alan's tone was airy but he watched her obliquely out of the corner of his eye.

"You didn't think it rot when I told you the name of our new boarder," said Sara. "Alan, you must have seen that programme. Why didn't you tell me about it last night?"

It looked for a moment as if he were going to deny all previous knowledge of the programme. If so he changed his mind. He shrugged his elegant shoulders. "Have a heart, Sara! Tell you what? That one of the fuddy-duddies was once the toast of Vienna? You'd have laughed in my face. What I did do was to stay up half the night keeping an eye on things. And this is all the thanks I get." He sounded aggrieved.

"All I'm saying is that you should have warned me. Then I should, at least, have been prepared."

Something in her tone of voice caught at his attention. "D'you mean *you* think there is something in this chap's story?"

"Mr. Carron seemed to think so. I rang him up and told him about it and he's coming round."

Alan was excited. "Then Kardos *is* down here to search for the Lake of Fire." The name seemed to run from them down the narrow passage, echoing eerily.

"Oh hush!" said Sara. She was conscious suddenly of the unwisdom of discussing the matter where they could be overheard. "Come into our room and close the door—tight."

She turned back as she spoke. She stood by her desk, pale, frowning, her melancholy profile thrown into relief by the gathering darkness.

Alan followed her. He was bubbling over with excitement. "But that's marvellous! Don't you see? Since the diamond really does exist, if Mr. Carron tells us which of the old girls is—or was—the errant Tamara we shall be half way to finding the stone."

Sara raised her head. She looked at him levelly. "And what good would that do?"

"Probably none." Alan perched himself on a corner of the desk and lighted a cigarette. "I suppose I want to know just for the devil of it. A sort of challenge." He looked at his sister through clouds of smoke. "Don't you feel it? The urge to join in? To do down this chap, Kardos, and all his lies?"

"No, I don't." Sara spoke wearily. "I just wish the whole thing were over. Or, better still, had never begun."

"Obviously it's no good wishing that. As for the business being over, when the diamond is found it *will* be over. There'll be no point then in Kardos hanging round." Alan slid off the desk with a businesslike air as if he were preparing to begin the search there and then. "You see if Mr. Carron doesn't agree with me. Since someone is going to find the diamond it had much better be one of us."

"Mr. Carron will probably want to call in the police."

"And tell them a story like that? Be your age, Sara." Alan was grinning. He looked very pleased with himself, very handsome and debonair. "I'm just going to dash out and get some cigarettes. I'll be back before the old boy gets here."

"And I must go and put on a frock. Mr. Carron doesn't care for trousers on women." She did not like the idea put forward so blithely by her young brother. She felt that he overestimated his ability. That he would be no match for the suave Mr. Kardos. There was a ruthlessness about him that seemed to mark him out as a dangerous man.

She went slowly along the shadowy passage and up the curving staircase. Somewhere out of sight behind her a stair creaked. She waited a moment but no one appeared. Somehow in her present mood and in this otherwise completely silent house, it was disturbing.

She paused in front of a mirror, half expecting to see another image appear beside her own in the grey green depth but none came. Only her own face looked back at her, pale, staring and a little anxious.

She went on up, half her attention behind her. She halted. Now there *was* someone on the stairs behind her.

"Miss Sara!" It was Mr. Gadsby coming up on long spidery legs. He peered closer. "What is the matter? You look quite pale."

"It must be a trick of the light." Absurd that she should still feel frightened. "Was there—did you see anyone else on the stairs?"

"No one. I came to tell you that I had left Mr. Carron in your office reading the paper."

"Thank you." Sara felt her smile stiff on her face.

Mr. Gadsby smiled his pale smile. "No need to hurry

yourself. I poked up the fire before I left to make the room comfortable."

Sara went on to her own room. As she hurried about her panic subsided. The knowledge that Mr. Carron was in the house was like a fresh breeze blowing away the cobwebs and mists of the past.

She ran down the stairs and along a passage now mercifully free of ghosts. She opened the door of the sitting room. It was full of golden firelight. The dancing flames masked the shabbiness of the furniture and lent a spurious gaiety to the faded decorations.

Mr. Carron was sitting in a wing armchair. His head had dropped onto his breast. The newspaper lay open across his knees.

"Mr. Carron!" she said and heard the thinness and alarm in her voice. She went nearer. She saw then that he was dead. Her throat seemed to close up. She could feel the tears pricking behind the eyelids. It was the excitement, she thought sadly. Hearing of Tamara Lubova must have come as a shock to him. It was too much for him at his age.

It was no time to think of herself—yet she could not help but do so. Now she was utterly alone. Her courage seemed to drain away from her. She couldn't bear it. She could not *begin* to bear it. Panic and desolation possessed her.

Alan burst exuberantly into the room. "Jolly good of you to come round, sir. I hope . . ." He broke off, peering shortsightedly through the flickering firelight. "What's the matter with him?"

"He's dead. I found him—like that."

"Dead? He can't be." An extraordinary change had come over Alan. His handsome face was distorted by passion. He picked up one flaccid hand, then threw it from him with a furious cry. "It's true. He is dead, curse him! Now we'll be no better off than the rest of the hunt."

Sara stared at him with horrified eyes. "Alan! How can you?"

"How can I?" He mimicked her savagely. "How can I—when I've just been robbed of the chance of a lifetime?" He banged a clenched fist frantically into the palm of his other hand. "If only he'd lived another half hour—a quarter even." He fell silent, gnawing his lower lip. His eyes roved about the room as if somewhere he would find some hint of the knowledge the old solicitor had taken with him to the grave.

He said suddenly, "I wonder if he brought any papers with him?" Renewed hope ran through his voice. "A letter or a document of some sort. Perhaps in his pocket." He pushed his sister aside. "Get out of my way, can't you?"

He bent over the dead man, ignoring Sara's low voiced, frantic sounding protests. His hand went out. He drew it back with a thin scream.

"What is it?" Sara asked, shuddering.

"I touched something. Something wet." His voice was a whisper. "Sara, turn on the lights."

She stumbled across the room. The room sprang into view, shabby furniture, framed theatrical posters on the walls, books, newspapers—every detail distinct in a hard clear light.

There was a dark stain on the cloth of Mr. Carron's waistcoat—and it was still growing.

"It's blood," Sara whispered. "On your hand too."

"He's been stabbed," said Alan, his breath whistling thinly in his throat. "While he was sitting there reading the paper someone stabbed him."

In sudden terror he looked into his sister's face, his eyes wild and staring, but saw only a reflection of his own terror. Speechless, not breathing, they stared at each other. While from the chair, the man who had been so staunch a friend watched through half closed lids, without kindness or favour.

Chapter 5

If Septimus Finch was surprised at the speed with which his prognostications had been fulfilled, and even more that they had been fulfilled at all, Slater was filled with gloom. So that it was with widely differing emotions that the two men arrived at the headquarters of the Seamarsh Constabulary.

Here they were met by Superintendent Enderby, a big man with a fat weather-beaten face, a straggling moustache and a balding head. With him was Mr. Ransome, the Chief Constable. He had a quiet restrained manner and his eyes were small and cold.

Both men spoke highly of the dead man's character. The murder was discussed. Finch examined photographs taken on the spot and glanced through Enderby's typewritten report.

"There is," said Mr. Ransome, "a secondary motive for murder. So slight a one that I only mention it to put you completely in the picture. Mr. Carron held a considerable mortgage on No. 9. Miss Harkness was six months behind with the interest and, as far as one can gather, had little chance of paying it."

"She is in financial difficulties? Surely the position would hardly be improved by Mr. Carron's death?"

"That's where you're wrong. I got on to his Managing Clerk. I learned that the will revokes all claim to money owed to him in any way. It mentions specifically the mortgage on No. 9, which ceases to exist as from the date of his death."

Finch nodded. "I see. Who else benefits from the will?"

"There are bequests to servants and to office staff, if still in his employ. Ten thousand pounds and his wife's jewellery to his niece, Mrs. Brooks. The residue goes to local charities." The Chief Constable added, "I must admit to preferring a straight-forward motive, such as financial benefit, rather than this story

59

of a missing diamond and a woman who was once mistress of an archduke.''

"And such a motive may be the right one,'' Finch agreed. "We haven't enough evidence at present to decide one way or the other. But for myself I'd far rather join in a game of hunt the diamond. Or spot the lady—even if she is dead.''

"We thought she must be dead,'' said Enderby. "Didn't seem much point in killing Mr. Carron otherwise.''

"No, Tamara Lubova was the legal owner of the diamond. She had nothing to fear on that score. Added to which she would have known that Mr. Carron would not have revealed the secret of her identity without her permission. Indeed the fact that he proposed to talk direct to Miss Harkness suggests that he could no longer do so with the woman most concerned. And finally isn't that what the writer of the letter wrote? *'The person you mentioned is dead.'?''*

"But it goes on *'and wishes to remain so,'* '' said Mr. Ransome triumphantly. "And that sounds as if it were only what one might call a symbolic death.''

Said Enderby with a chuckle, "She could hardly write what she really meant. The person you mentioned is dead and I have the diamond, so kindly mind your own business.''

"If Kardos is as smart as I think he is,'' said Finch drily, "he'll be reading it in that sense by now.'' He added, "How long elapsed between Mr. Carron's arrival and Miss Harkness' discovery of the murder?''

"She says she must have been a good five minutes in her bedroom, probably more.''

"And this Mr. Gadsby who opened the door to Mr. Carron?''

"He taught painting for years at the local art school. A curiously colourless man.'' It was Enderby who answered. "Paints curiously colourless seascapes. You can see some of them hanging in the downstairs sitting room at No. 9. Old Mr. Harkness was his only patron. Or the only one I ever heard of.'' Adding dubiously, "He could have killed Mr. Carron, of course, but I find it a bit difficult to imagine his doing anything as positive.''

"The idea's absurd to anyone who knows the man,'' declared Mr. Ransome. "No, my idea is that the murderer went down the back stairs. Daisy Apps, the maid, was in the lounge clearing away the tea things. She says she didn't hear or see anyone pass through the hall. Now did she hear the lift working.''

"Is she to be trusted?''

"I imagine so. Mr. Harkness provided for her in his will

but she refused to leave his widow. At her death she transferred her allegiance to Miss Harkness. Admittedly she's an odd character but her affection and loyalty have always been fixed on the Harkness family."

"And she found the murder weapon lying in the sink?"

"Yes. She says she knew nothing of the murder until she passed the office with the tea trolley and Miss Harkness called her in. When she went on into the kitchen, there was a knife lying in a pool of pinkish water." Enderby added wryly, "She was still having hysterics when I got there ten minutes later."

"No finger prints, of course?"

"I doubt if the knife would have taken any. It had a rough black horn handle. In fact it was ideally suited to the murderer's purpose. The blade had been worn by constant use to a length of seven and a half inches. It was thin as a wafer and sharp as a razor."

Finch nodded. "A murder done on the spur of the moment. They're usually madly easy to solve or profoundly difficult. Tell me, who started this guest house and why?"

"That goes back quite a way," said Enderby, since the Chief Constable seemed to have withdrawn from the conversation. "Mr. Harkness loathed the Nazis and all their works. Most of all, he loathed their racial discrimination. He became, in spite of his age, a sort of Scarlet Pimpernel; with the result that No. 9 was soon full of refugees. With the war over they tended to drift away or go back to their own country until, in the end, only Madame Rakosi and Madame Kosetti were left of the original number. After Mr. Harkness died in 1949 his widow began it all over again but with people with whom she had more in common. The McGees, old friends of her husband's, who could quite well have afforded to live in an hotel, and Mr. Gadsby. Mrs. Bradshaw, whose husband had been Mr. Harkness' managing clerk; Mrs. Winfield, a parson's widow, and Miss Millamont whose father was a local vicar."

Finch raised a quizzical eyebrow. "A laudable work on Mr. Harkness' part—but still, I seem to detect a faint note of reserve in your voice."

"You do?" Enderby looked abashed. "The fact is that Mr. Harkness left his considerable fortune to his widow for life and then it went to various charitable international bodies. Not a pennypiece to Seamarsh and he a local man, born and bred. It caused quite a bit of feeling at the time."

"So that's it?" Finch glanced down at Enderby's report. "You don't seem to have got far with the old people."

Enderby rolled his eyes in an affectation of despair. "Those three old ladies! They'd say nothing. Just sat like images. Or rather two of 'em sat. The third, Madame Kosetti, remained in bed. All sixteen stone of her. And not a word could I get out of one of them. They must have agreed on it beforehand."

"You say *three* old ladies?"

"The fourth, Miss Millamont, is following a different line. She's bolted herself into her bedroom and refuses to come out. Says she's staying there until the murderer is caught and would someone please bring her a couple of raw shell eggs at regular intervals."

"What's she planning to do with them?"

"Eat 'em." The Chief Constable joined in abruptly. "She says even the Borgias couldn't find a way of poisoning shell eggs without detection." He gave a harsh bark that Finch realised was meant for laughter.

On that note the meeting would have broken up had not Finch, as he was leaving, paused to ask, "By the way, just what, or who, are the Watchful People?"

"It's a purely local sect," said Enderby, who had accompanied him to the door. "It was started by a man called Jolly. His father owned a chain of drapers' shops all along the coast. A successful business man and as confirmed a Seventh Day Adventist as you could hope to find. When he died his son sold the shops and founded the Chapel of the Watchful People with himself as High Priest, or whatever you like to call it. That was forty years ago. I fancy it would have folded up at his death if he hadn't endowed it so handsomely. We've never had any complaints but I can't say I know what goes on there."

"I can tell you," said the Chief Constable. "They're waiting for the end of the world—only waiting in a state of extreme comfort." His laugh that was so like the rasping of a rusty hinge followed Finch down the passage.

It was ten minutes to nine when the police car drew up in Belmont Square. It was very still now. A cold mist drifted in from the sea and the lamps were wreathed in shifting vapour. The sodium lighting had taken all colour from the scene and the shifting crowd of curious onlookers had the pallid look of a company of ghosts.

No. 9 itself appeared grim, shabby and forlorn. Two dimen-

sional, with windows glittering like steel and not a light showing. A young uniformed constable opened the door. He seemed
relieved to see them.

Septimus Finch looked curiously about him. It was so right
for period that for an instant the young Tamara, gay, witty and
acquisitive, seemed in the room with him. He caught the echo of
ghostly laughter, glitter of uniforms and tight-fitting cavalry
boots. Jewels on a smooth white bosom and a small hand
fingering a flawless diamond. And now? Had it all come down
to this? A kitchen knife and the callous murder of a harmless old
man?

"Everything quiet?"

"Yes, sir."

"Where are they all?"

"Mr. Kardos is with Mr. Gadsby in the lounge and has
been ever since supper. The others all went upstairs—except the
maid. She helped Miss Harkness clear away and then took the
things on a trolley back to the kitchen." Adding rather anxiously
as if the very fact might constitute a dereliction of duty, "I
haven't seen anyone since."

"How about Mrs. Brooks?"

"She didn't come down to supper. Too upset. Miss Harkness
took a tray up to her room."

Which seemed, Finch reflected, more or less, to account for
everyone. He asked to be shown where the murder had taken
place.

It was stark cold and had lost whatever air of comfort it
might have had before the old solicitor's demise. Grey ash filled
the grate. Curtains and carpet showed threadbare. There was a
damp patch below the solitary window and the brightly coloured
posters that did duty as pictures stood out with a garish
unsuitability.

A big winged chair in an old Holland cover was drawn up
before the now extinct fire.

Finch moved round to stand between this and the fireplace.
"The murderer must have stood about here," he murmured,
recalling the photographs of the dead man. "Probably made
some remark about the cold to justify his having done so. The
old gentleman would have put down his newspaper, prepared for
a little light conversation. And, in its place, got a knife through
his guts. A nasty business." He tried a drawer of the rather
battered kneehole desk. "Wonder if any of old Mrs. Harkness'
papers are extant? We shall have to have a search, both here and

at Mr. Carron's office. Not much good looking in his pockets. The murderer has probably searched them already.''

"Let's hope Mr. Carron didn't carry the only information round in his head," said Slater.

"There is that danger." Finch turned to the door. "There's nothing to see here." He went into the passage.

The stairs, some six feet from the office door, opened straight onto the passage. They were in darkness. Finch found and turned on the light switch. At once the quiet was broken by the sound of running footsteps. Someone had been on the stairs out of sight round the bend. Someone who had been standing in the darkness, listening and now, on agile feet, was speeding away.

Slater gave chase.

The lights on the stairs went out again. The passage beyond was plunged into darkness. By the time Slater's groping hand had found the light switch there was no one in sight.

A young woman appeared suddenly hurrying round a corner. A plain, hollow cheeked young woman, in a grey woollen frock. She was thin as a rake but her long legs, decided Slater, who fancied himself as a connoisseur, were spectacular. As she drew near he saw that her eyes held a bemused look as if she were suffering from shock.

"Did anyone pass you in the passage?" Slater asked.

"No-one." She looked at him levelly out of grey eyes surrounded by thick stubby lashes. "What's going on? And who are you?"

"I'm Detective Sergeant Slater. As for what's going on I caught someone listening on the stairs, but whoever it was had the forethought to turn out the lights. That slowed me down considerably. By the time I'd managed to turn them on again the passage was empty."

Sara shivered, hugging herself with thin arms. "There seems to have been someone skulking about in the house all day," she said. Her voice showed a tendency to die away as if from sheer exhaustion.

She looked past him down the passage as she spoke. Bending her head a little so that her face seemed all angles and blue shadows. A study in anatomy, Slater reflected, taking a mental inventory. Fine pale skin, no lipstick, very little powder. Nice hands but scarred and work-worn. Why doesn't she wear gloves? he wondered impatiently.

"D'you mean you've heard someone about?" he asked.

"Before Mr. Carron came I heard someone coming up the stairs behind me. I waited but no one appeared. Perhaps I imagined it but I don't think so."

Slater frowned a little. Damn it, the girl did look a mess. "What you want," he said encouragingly, "is a good booze up. But not, of course, until after you've seen my chief."

As he went down the stairs he wondered if he should have left her. She seemed somehow so much in need of help and protection.

He looked back and saw her still standing in an attitude of tense expectancy as if she were waiting for someone to appear suddenly before her in the shadowy corridors.

He found Finch in the kitchen, a big room dusky in the far corners and stuffily warm with the smell of cooked food. He was talking to a sour faced woman whose air of bleak respectability was somewhat counteracted by a wild eye and an unnatural pallor. She wore a black frock, a dark apron pinned over a small fancy one and a cap. Her frock had a neat turned down collar pinned with a silver brooch.

"The mistress gave me a holiday in the New Year," she was saying, her thin voice raised above the noise of washing up. "And a nice holiday it proved. I went to Kings Lynn, to my married sister and fell ill there. Caught 'flu and was pretty bad. Couldn't even get back for the mistress's funeral. Me, who was nearer to her than anyone."

She paused to put three saucepans on a shelf. Bang, bang they went and the lids jangled as she piled them briskly one on top of the other.

"When I came back I found everything in a nice state. Muddle and waste everywhere, the old ladies ruling the roost and poor Miss Sara at her wit's end."

"The old ladies took advantage of her, did they?" As Finch watched Daisy whisking about so competently, on her match-stick legs, he began to see how it was that the house managed to look so clean and well polished.

"That they did." Daisy swished out the water in the sink. "But there, the mistress should never have left the place to Miss Sara and so I told her. The money was no more than a bribe but she couldn't see any harm in it. The way the master had left things she couldn't provide for the old people in any other way. But the truth is she knew how to handle them. If you don't like it, you can go somewhere else, she'd say. And that would settle it. But not Miss Sara. If it hadn't been for me that thousand

pounds would have gone even faster than it did. Paying for
Master Alan's fads and fancies and not for what was wanted in
the house. New carpets, covers, curtains. If I hadn't spent hours
repairing them they wouldn't even hang up, as it is you daren't
ever draw them.''

Daisy was still a moment, her narrow back to Finch. "He's
a bad one that brother of hers," she said at length without
turning. "It's no good her having any money. He'd only take it
off her.''

Finch was surprised at the amount of feeling in her voice.
"Did you see anything of Mr. Kardos' television appearance?"

"I did and I didn't, as you might say. That was the evening
Mrs. Brooks upset the coffee. I'd just knocked and taken it into
her room. I heard someone mention a diamond—a Stone of Fire,
or some such fancy name—when Mrs. Brooks sprang up and
over went the tray. Coffee everywhere. So there I was cleaning
up whilst that Mr. Kardos was carrying on, staring out like a
hypnotist at a fair.''

"It's an odd thought," Finch commented. "But it does
seem possible that the stone is here.''

Daisy sniffed. "It's possible, I suppose," she admitted
grudgingly. "Mr. Harkness was always a great one for lost
causes. We've had foreigners in and out of the house since
before the last war, and they were all hoarders. One of them
might have hoarded a diamond—but I can't say any of them
looked the part.'' She closed her lips into a thin repressive line.

"Did any of them look the part of Tamara Lubova?"

"Not unless it was that Madame Rakosi. She charmed
everyone, except me. Used to turn it on and off like a tap. Or
there's Madame Kosetti. She's had money in the past. You can
always tell. But where it used to come from I don't know. The
first I ever heard of her was when the master told me to make up
the bed in the best spare room. She was in the house already but
how she got here I don't know to this day.''

"You've been here a long time, haven't you?"

Daisy was busy putting the breakfast things, cutlery and
china, on the trolley in preparation for next day's breakfast. She
paused to look at him. "Nearly thirty years. The master was a
bachelor then. He used to go away always for Christmas and stay
in an hotel. And one year, that would have been 1935, he went
to Torquay. That's where he found his wife. She was a doctor's
widow. He'd left no money and she was working as a reception-
ist with another doctor. A real romance!'' From her acid tone

Finch gathered that she didn't hold with romance but here, perhaps, he was wrong.

Daisy added, "But maybe it was a romance at that. She was in her forties when she married the master. Real nice-looking— an outdoor type. Not a beauty mind you, but nice-looking. She was born somewhere down Devonshire way. She used to talk about it to me." Daisy had ceased working. She was staring unseeingly in front of her and her voice was fond. "Such queer things she missed. The wind and the Atlantic rollers. Even the rivers in these parts were too placid for her liking."

"I understand that after Mr. Harkness' death the number of people in the house dwindled?"

"Yes. The mistress wasn't as liberal as the master had been, and gradually they drifted away. After they'd gone she missed them. Leastways she missed having people round her. 'Damn this silence, Daisy,' she'd say to me. 'It's absolutely deafening.' So then *she* looked round for people who needed a home, but who were more congenial like."

The kitchen was tidy now. The trolley piled high. Daisy took off her apron and slipped into her coat.

"And only Madame Kosetti and Madame Rakosi remained of the original guests?"

"That's it, sir." Daisy spoke with brief finality. "I'm going out now."

"To the chapel?"

She was buttoning her coat. "There are only two days left." There was a curiously rapt and inward stare in her eyes, as if she were consulting some intelligence other than her own. *"These things saith he that hath the seven Spirits of God and the seven stars: If therefore thou shalt not watch I will come on thee as a thief and thou shalt not know what hour I will come upon thee."*

She turned away and, with the celerity with which she did everything, opened the kitchen door and slipped through. The two C.I.D. men heard the back door open, then close behind her.

"Did you see her brooch?" Finch asked, a phantom expression of pleasure flitting across his face.

"Not clearly, sir. It had a name on it in silver letters, didn't it?"

"Not a name. Just the single word 'Satisfied.' "

Slater gave a muffled snort of amusement. "But what does it mean? What's she got to be satisfied about?"

"The end of the world, I suppose. And I must say it's big hearted of her."

The two men walked down the passage.

"How did you get on, Archie?"

Slater told him.

"So Miss Harkness held you up, did she? Then it must have been her brother you chased. That's one mystery solved."

This aspect of their meeting had not occurred to Slater. He did not like it. He would have sworn that Sara Harkness was incapable of guile and double dealing.

Chapter 6

Septimus Finch looked at Sara with interest. A nice face, he thought. Intelligent too and he recalled with amusement how she had fooled his sergeant.

Like Slater he saw that she was suffering from shock but there was more to it than that. She seemed almost sullen—offended. As if someone had done her a great injury. Perhaps she felt that Mr. Carron had done so by dying. It was an intriguing thought.

She had pushed some of the tables back in the dining room to clear a space in front of the fire. She had taken the white damask cloths off the two remaining tables and placed a comfortably padded chair to each.

Slater refused his. He insisted that Sara use it herself. "I'm going to take down what's said," he explained to her. "I shall get on better in one of the higher, straight-backed chairs."

At Finch's réquest Sara began her account from the time of the arrival of Istvan Kardos. She told it stumblingly at first, forgetting things and having to go back. But soon, she was speaking lucidly, recalling details that she had scarcely known that she had noticed at the time. It was a relief to tell someone all—or almost all—that had troubled her during the last twenty-four hours.

She found reassurance too in Finch's presence. This was partly due to mere physical size. Partly because he entered so much into her story, expressing amazement with the raising of an eyebrow. Horror with a drooping lip. It took her some time to discover that he was actually enjoying himself.

For his part Finch judged her to be completely candid, except where her brother was concerned. When she spoke of him her voice slowed a little as if she were picking her words.

Slater, in the background, thought that she had a gift for

sitting still. Her very quietness, he decided critically, had a quality of its own.

As Sara came to her discovery of Mr. Carron's dead body, tension came back to her. Her voice grew thin and strained. Her mouth was distorted in a grimace of grief and horror.

"You were fond of him?" Finch asked.

She nodded. "And it isn't only that. I know it's no time to think of myself but I can't help wondering how I'm going to get on without him. He was so—wise and, oh, endlessly kind. If you felt you couldn't do what he suggested he didn't just wash his hands of you. He'd sit down and work out some other plan that you felt you could carry out."

Finch heaved a commiserating sigh. His expression was dolorous. "Your maid, Daisy, seems very fond of you," he offered.

Sara smiled crookedly. "But not in a comfortable way. I'm afraid I never quite come up to her expectations. She's rather like a hair shirt, always telling me where I'm wrong. At the moment she's more depressing than usual."

"According to her in two days' time you should be back to normal—or the end of the world will have come and none of this will matter."

From Sara's face he gathered that, as far as she was concerned, the end of the world could come any time it liked.

"When did the household know that Mr. Kardos was coming here?"

"Daisy knew from the beginning. It was her idea that I write and put him off. It doesn't really pay to have a temporary visitor in the winter, particularly a man. It adds so much to the expenses. You see, Mrs. Brooks is out for a lot of meals. That leaves only the fuddy-duddies to cater for."

"And when did they know about Mr. Kardos?"

"Only on the morning of his arrival. They're apt to resent the arrival of strangers, particularly in the winter. Besides they're so inquisitive." She broke off, then added slowly, "At least, generally they're inquisitive. This time, except for Miss Millamont, they didn't say anything. Just went on with their breakfasts."

"You think now that they were expecting—or, at any rate, were prepared for the announcement?"

"All but Miss Millamont, yes." She added belatedly, "And of course, Mr. Gadsby. He never says anything." Finch nodded. Always the old ladies and Mr. Gadsby as an afterthought. He said aloud, "How about Mrs. Brooks?"

"I didn't tell her at all. This is just an hotel to her. Not home, as it is to the old people."

"And how did they learn of Mr. Carron's death?"

"They came down when they heard Daisy screaming. It was—terrible. Magda Brooks in a state of collapse. Daisy in hysterics and Miss Millamont giving little shrieks of alarm like a train whistling. Mr. Kardos——" She broke off, her face hardening a little.

"Yes?" Finch prompted her.

Said Sara reluctantly, "He seemed angry. He accused me of not understanding. Of not taking his story seriously enough. Then Madame Kosetti got very angry and they added to the general din by shrieking at each other in some foreign language. I don't know what they said but I think they were calling each other names."

"Had you sent for the police?"

"Yes. Alan rang them up as soon as we discovered that Mr. Carron had been stabbed."

Finch nodded. "Who answers the front door as a rule?"

"Whoever is near at the time." Sara added, "But not Mrs. Bradshaw, although she isn't above peering out of the window to see who is there. She says Gordon, that's her husband, didn't expect her to answer the door at home and that he doesn't like her to do it here. And anyway usually it's Mr. Gadsby because of his habit of sitting in the hall."

"He likes to see what goes on, does he?"

Sara hesitated, frowning a little. "It's a bit difficult to say. The old have so few diversions. Books are too heavy, newspapers soon tire them. They can't walk far. So many of their activities are prompted simply by a desire to pass the time."

"Like Miss Millamont slipping into the old people's home to watch television?"

"She watches the trains come in too—and the buses going in and out. But she likes the trains best, particularly in the summer when there's all the bustle of visitors coming and going."

"You mentioned Mrs. Bradshaw's husband but I see the Superintendent put her down as a widow?"

"She is a widow. I don't know when she began it but ever since I've known her she has behaved as if he were still alive. Daisy says that when he *was* alive they both wanted to be boss and used to quarrel dreadfully. Now he's dead she lays down the law and he simply agrees with her." Sara added wearily, "I think it isn't so much affection that makes her pretend he's still with her, as a sort of spiritual revenge.''

"She's got the better of him at last. Is that it? She doesn't sound a very amiable character.''

"I wouldn't mind if he wouldn't back her up when she accuses Miss Millamont of taking her things.''

Finch looked at her quizzically. "But she does take things, doesn't she?''

"Only little things.'' Sara's voice was defensive. "And she puts them back again. I remember once I brought back a tinsel star from some party or other. I left it lying on my dressing table and at supper next day Miss Millamont was wearing it in her hair. I didn't say anything. I thought it rather pathetic. Then, when I woke up one morning a few days later, there it was. Back on my dressing table, exactly where it had been before.''

"You mean, Miss Millamont had come into your room during the night?'' Finch's voice was purposely unemphatic. For all that, with the words, some change seemed to come into the atmosphere.

"Yes, I don't lock my door.'' Sara laughed a little uneasily. "As a matter of fact, it hasn't a key.''

"Do all the old people wander about at night?''

"Oh yes.'' Sara tried to speak carelessly. "At their age they don't want much sleep.'' Then indignation forced its way into her voice. "I think that's just silly. Miss Millamont is a romantic. She lives in a world of her own. I can't imagine her harming anyone.''

"Can you imagine any of them sticking a knife into a harmless old gentleman? But someone in this house did, you know.''

Sara frowned, biting her lips. It was true. While she had been in her bedroom murder had crept unsuspected into the prosaic surroundings of the office—just as Miss Millamont had crept into her bedroom to return a tinsel star. Murder had reached out from the shadows just as Miss Millamont might have. . . .

She pushed the thought from her. She began speaking quickly, colour coming into her face. "What you're really saying is that I don't know them. I quite realise that fact. I've realised it ever since I spoke to Mr. Carron. I *don't* know them. For all *I* know they may have been passing the diamond about as they passed Madame Rakosi's collection of foreign novels. . . .'' She became aware of the rising note of hysteria in her voice. She closed her lips firmly and was silent, staring straight in front of her, a bitter expression on her face.

Finch said nothing for a moment. So that's it, he was thinking. That's why she looks so dazed and lost. And it was the old ladies who had injured her by their secrecy and not Mr. Carron at all. They had made her feel of no account and the sacrifice of her youth as nothing.

He said aloud in his soft drawl, "Madame Rakosi? Tell me about her."

"She was one of the old ladies who died. She . . ." Sara broke off while dismay spread across her face. "I've just remembered. Talking of Madame Rakosi's death brought it back to me. It was just after it happened. I was in her bedroom. It was getting dark and I was standing at the window opposite the door. Suddenly I saw the handle turning. Then the door opened, very slowly and without a sound and there she was. Miss Millamont I mean. She looked so queer—as if she were in a trance. And there was such a silly smile on her face. She saw me and, just as quietly, closed the door again. It—it was all rather like a dream— the darkness and Madame Rakosi lying dead on the bed. Only it wasn't a dream. I remember I collected all her really personal things, letters and bits of jewellery and locked them up in the desk in my office."

"Who was Madame Rakosi?"

"She was an Austrian, a widow. Her husband had been in the Austrian army. I did think that perhaps *she* might have been Tamara Lubova. You could see she'd been beautiful."

Finch nodded. "What did you do eventually with the things you'd locked up?"

"I sent the jewellery off to a nephew in Leipzig. And I burnt the letters in the boiler."

Finch's eyebrows rose. "Unread?"

Sara nodded. "Not even taken out of their envelopes, I'm afraid. But I did notice that they all had foreign stamps, and that they looked awfully old. Actually no one here gets many letters. Madame Kosetti comes off best. Relations write to tell her about funerals and weddings and who's had a baby."

"Wonder if they're her husband's relations?" said Finch. "But we can find out all that. Tell me more about Madame Rakosi. Daisy said she died of pneumonia."

"Yes. It was in the spring of 1959. Everything seemed to go wrong just then. The weather was atrocious. Madame Rakosi managed to catch cold and it settled on her lungs. She hated the idea of going into hospital and as the doctor didn't hold out much hope for her, there didn't seem any point in sending her away.''

"You nursed her?"

"Yes, she was an awfully good patient. She knew she was dying but she was quite cheerful and undismayed. I remember her laughing and saying that she wouldn't divide up her things while she was still alive as the old ladies would get much more fun fighting over them after she'd gone—and she was right.''

"But if she'd had the diamond wouldn't she have mentioned it before she died?"

"Perhaps she did to someone else." The sullen look was back on Sara's face. "Or perhaps she would have done if she hadn't suddenly become much worse and lost consciousness.''

"Had she any particular friend?"

"She used to talk to Mr. McGee a lot. And she liked Mr. Carron but she didn't care for women much. She said they bored her." Sara added, "But when she was ill, she did see quite a lot of a Mrs. Winfield. She was a parson's widow. A miserable creature. Always creeping about in carpet slippers and wrapped in an enormous black knitted shawl. She didn't approve of Madame Rakosi but she said it was her Christian duty to visit her. I'd have stopped her only she seemed to amuse Madame Rakosi.''

Sara fell silent, frowning a little. "I remember her saying to me, 'That ugly depressing woman to come and talk to me of sin. To me, who has been a happy sinner all my life. I shock her very much. I shock her far more than I shock your nice clergyman whose business it is to be shocked.' "

"Now that is interesting; for if Madame Rakosi told Mrs. Winfield about her past she may well have told her—or, at any rate, hinted at her possession of the diamond. It would have been just the sort of story to horrify a narrow minded woman such as Mrs. Winfield appears to have been." Finch glanced down at the list of names Enderby had given him. "Her name isn't here. Don't tell me she's dead?"

"Yes, she died about a fortnight after Madame Rakosi. She'd had a bad heart for some time and was liable to drop dead at any moment. Actually it happened in the lift. She must have felt an attack coming on for she managed to stop it. . . .'' Again Sara broke off. She stared at Finch whilst horror widened her eyes and thinned her voice.

"Remembered something else?"

Sara nodded. She said slowly, "When she was found her face wore such a look of terror that even the doctor was shocked. Mr. McGee said that she looked as if she'd been frightened to death."

"He did, did he? And what's happened to him?"

Said Sara in a voice that was only a thread of sound, "He fell downstairs and broke his neck five days after Mrs. Winfield's death."

There followed a moment's paralysing silence.

Finch ended it. "Rather an odd sequence of events, don't you think?" he asked mildly.

For answer Sara bent her head and burst into peals of half stifled laughter. For a moment the two men were alarmed, thinking that they had a case of hysterics on their hands. Then they realised that, however misplaced, it was genuine amusement, if of a rather wild nature.

Presently Sara raised her head. "Oh dear! How dreadful of me. I do apologise but really I couldn't help it." She wiped her eyes. Meeting the sympathetic and mildly appreciative gaze of the two men she seemed for a moment in danger of going off again. When she could control her voice she said, "There was I wallowing in self-pity. Cut to the quick because the old ladies hadn't confided in me. And all the t-time they c-couldn't because they'd been m-murdering each other. O-oh!"

She pressed her handkerchief against her mouth and looked above it at the C.I.D. men with such brilliant laughing eyes that Slater caught himself thinking she was beautiful. This took him by surprise and put him off his work for a time.

"Actually," said Finch in tones of faint reproof, "it's a pretty bad business."

"I know," agreed Sara meekly, with a last exhausted hiccup.

"Let's take Mrs. Winfield's death first. Who found her?"

"Alan—my brother. He was going up to see Mrs. Brooks." Finch fancied that he detected a faint edge to her voice. Jealous? It would not be surprising. "He had to walk up because the lift was stuck somewhere. He thought one of the old ladies had left it, with the door open, on the second floor, but there it was, on the first, and poor old Mrs. Winfield lying dead inside it."

"Right inside?"

"Yes—sort of huddled in one corner."

"The corner nearest to the control panel?"

"N-no. The opposite one." Sara was serious enough now,

even distressed but not, Finch noted with satisfaction, more than was natural.

"Did her death occasion any talk?"

"Everyone was horrified, of course. But that isn't what you mean, is it?" Sara thought for a moment. Then she said, "I remember Daisy asking me if I hadn't thought that Mrs. Winfield had had something on her mind. But, of course, she wasn't thinking of murder. Just that worry might have contributed to her death."

"And had you thought so?"

"No—but then Daisy knew her better than I did."

"Right. I'll talk to her about it. Now let's get on to Mr. McGee. Who found *him*?"

"I did. I'd gone down the back stairs to answer the telephone. I remember that because someone wanted to speak to Mr. Gadsby. And whoever it was must have got awfully tired of waiting because when I went into the hall to find Mr. Gadsby there was Mr. McGee. I didn't remember the call until hours later."

"Can you remember whether it was a man or a woman speaking?"

"A man I think. It was a sort of thick voice. As if the speaker had a bad cold."

"Was Mr. Gadsby expecting a call?"

"No, he worried about it for weeks afterwards. You see he hardly ever had a telephone call."

"So the caller didn't ring again?"

Sara shook her head. She looked anxiously at Finch, wondering why he was so interested in this particular aspect of the affair.

"What did the doctor say about Mr. McGee's death?"

"That he'd broken his neck. And that he'd been dead about an hour."

"An hour? No one passed through the hall for an hour?"

"It wasn't really so unusual. It was an awful day. Raining and blowing. No one wanted to go out. And, anyway, the old people hardly ever use the public rooms. They wouldn't even come down for tea if I'd let them make it upstairs."

"Was there any suspicion of foul play?"

"No. People just thought this must be a very badly run place, but that was all." Sara hesitated. "Mrs. McGee has awful fits of remorse about something. Alan says it's because *she* pushed her husband down the stairs." Sara explained about Mrs.

McGee's gambling propensities, and the sense of guilt that periodically overcame her.

"How long has she been like that?"

"Only since her husband's death." Sara hesitated. Then she burst out, "Oh, but she couldn't have had anything to do with it. They quarrelled over these investments Mrs. McGee wanted to make—at least, she'd get very angry and storm at him but he seemed to take it all in his stride. But they were fond of each other. I *know* they were."

"What sort of man was he?"

"He was a very nice man. Very shrewd and businesslike but kind too. He used to keep the books and do my income tax for me. You see, with an invalid wife, he couldn't get out often or go away, and that left him without much to do except take an interest in what went on here."

Sara saw the implication of what she had said almost as soon as the words were spoken. Her face whitened so much that, for a moment, Finch feared that she was going to faint. A queer dead silence had fallen on the room.

When Sara did speak it was to say, wonderingly, "How patient you have to be once you've killed someone—and how watchful. All these months—years really. Alert for any sign of danger, the merest breath of suspicion——" She added with a great deal of self-reproach, "I don't seem to have been very bright, do I?"

Finch was shocked. "My dear girl, it isn't your place to go round suspecting crime. It isn't even safe. No, you keep out of it unless we ask for your help. Which reminds me, if there's any papers, letters or even housekeeping books belonging to Mrs. Harkness, you might let me have them."

"After her death I packed everything of hers away in trunks in one of the rooms in the attics."

"Then please give my sergeant the keys and he'll go through them. There may be something there that'll give us some clue as to Tamara Lubova's identity. But don't try and find out the answer for yourself. The murderer, as you've just said, will be watching every move made in this house. And, now we've rumbled him, he doesn't have so many things to worry about—except to make sure it's a dead body he leaves behind him."

A silence followed Sara's going from the room. Both men were busy with their own thoughts, thoughts that were not following the same channel.

"So Kardos didn't start something," said Finch reflectively.

"He simply resurrected it and, whatever the motive for Mr. Carron's murder—and Sara Harkness' evidence had left me with some reservations, at least as far as her brother is concerned, I don't think that there can be much doubt why Mrs. Winfield and Mr. McGee were murdered.

"And who *was* Tamara Lubova? Was it Madame Rakosi? Or was it merely coincidence that Mrs. Winfield was murdered shortly after the other woman's death? Everyone in this house is ideally situated to spy on everyone else and none, I imagine, was better equipped for the pastime than Mrs. Winfield, creeping silently about in bedroom slippers and wrapped in the impenetrability of a black shawl. And she wasn't the sort to be bribed or frightened into holding her tongue. Always supposing that someone hadn't discovered that *she* had the diamond. And if she did have it where is it now? Has Miss Millamont got it? Is that the real reason she has bolted herself into her bedroom? And did she get it, not from Mrs. Winfield, but from Madame Rakosi's room at a later date? And was it she who entered the lift with the unfortunate Mrs. Winfield in so horrible and threatening a guise that her victim died between one floor and the next?"

Finch broke off to peer at his sergeant. He was fond of talking and, lacking an audience, had been known to talk to himself with very much the effect of a large bee buzzing. But when he had an audience, particularly a junior colleague, he expected him to attend.

"Archie, you're not listening." Finch's expression was eloquent of pained surprise.

Slater came to with a start. "I was thinking about Mr. McGee," he declared untruthfully. Adding firmly "Mr. McGee and the telephone call."

"Yes, now, that is interesting. The bogus telephone call."

"Bogus?" Slater's attention was caught now. "I hadn't thought of it like that."

"Then consider it now. A telephone call made by someone in what appears to have been a disguised voice. Made to Mr. Gadsby who never gets telephone calls—but who does make a practice of sitting in the hall. So much so that anyone searching for him would go there first. And, in this case, find, not Mr. Gadsby, but a defunct Mr. McGee. But why this haste? Nerves? I wouldn't have suspected it."

"To throw someone down the stairs isn't a very certain way of killing them," said Slater. "And, I would have thought, a bit beyond an elderly person."

"Not," said Finch, "if it were preceded by a blow on the head and followed by the placing of one of the many plump cushions, which I noticed in the hall, over the unconscious person's face."

Chapter 7

Alan Harkness came into the room, graceful, elegant, far more handsome than either man had expected. He seemed quite at his ease. He sat back in the chair Finch indicated, and took out a handsome cigarette case which he offered to Finch before lighting one for himself with an equally handsome lighter. Then he subjected the detective to an almost insolent scrutiny. Slater he ignored.

This left the sergeant free to register his disgust. The smooth untroubled face, the fine hands, so like—and yet so unlike—his sister's. The general air of well being. The suit, obviously not off the peg, the expensive shirt, cuff links, tie and socks, all were offensive to Archie Slater.

Alan admitted coolly—and in a very pleasant speaking voice—to having seen Kardos' television appearance at a friend's house in London. He denied believing that it could be the same man, even when his sister had told him the name of her latest boarder.

He had, of course, recognised him when he had gone into the lounge to make a fourth at bridge. "Quite put me off my game," he said languidly. "I revoked twice and was madly unpopular." He told how he had kept a watch that night. Until half-past three, he said, but there Finch thought he exaggerated.

He had an alibi for the time of Mr. Carron's murder. "The girl at the tobacconist will remember me," he declared complacently. He had had no idea that the old boy had been murdered until he had turned on the light to see whether anything could be done for him. He added that Mr. Carron had held a mortgage on No. 9, adding ruefully that Heaven knew what would happen now.

"Your sister was very fond of Mr. Carron, I believe?"

"Yes. He was a father-figure to her. We lost our own when Sara was seven."

80

"You are in debt?"

"Not at the moment. Of course I was mad, but quite mad, to come down here in the first place. To live in Seamarsh is to be artistically dead. Then it's a jolly sight more expensive living here and having to go up and down to London. But Sara didn't want to come along. So here I am. No use repining."

He blew a cloud of blue smoke, smiled charmingly through it at Finch and never knew how close he came to being brained by Slater.

"Things seldom turn out as we expect," said Finch sententiously. Adding, "When you returned from the tobacconist, did you see or hear anything suspicious?"

"Nothing—but, of course, any one of the fuddy-duddies could have known that Mr. Carron was coming round and why. They spend hours listening at the telephone extension on the second floor. I know, for they sometimes display an almost embarrassing knowledge of my affairs." He shrugged elegantly, smiled faintly. "But who am I to grudge it them. Poor old things! Their love life is long past."

"And who would you fancy as the killer?" Finch asked. If there was an edge of sarcasm in his voice it passed his listener by.

"W-well!" Alan took up a judicial pose. "Obviously after Miss Millamont's story to my sister this morning, *she* can't be discounted. She's by no means the innocent we believed." He cocked a deep blue eye at Finch. "My sister told you that she's a thief?"

"She did."

Alan looked momentarily floored. "There you are then." He blew a couple of smoke rings. Watched them float, disintegrate. Then he said, "Of course, if Mr. Carron had been strangled I should have suggested that you paid special attention to Mrs. McGee. I don't suppose you've seen her yet but she has the muscles of a blacksmith and her hands. . . ." He shuddered affectedly. "And if anyone tells you she's helpless because her legs are withered, don't you believe it. I met her once, coming along the passage like a snake. A revolting sight. It's still my favourite nightmare."

He had one more contribution to make. He made it at the door as he went out. "I don't suppose it's of any importance but Magda Brooks had been quarrelling with her uncle. I've heard them just by chance. You know! On the stairs. Or when they've been standing at the door of her suite. Never enough to know

what it was all about, but I do know Magda's as hard to move as
a mule. And she's one of those women who know their way
about. That's why I was so amazed this evening when she broke
down as she did.''

"Have you heard them quarrelling lately?"

"The last time was two days ago—Monday afternoon. I
happened to be coming down the stairs behind them. I heard old
Carron say, 'I'm getting a little tired of this, Magda. I warn you,
if you won't do anything to right matters, then I will.' I made a
noise then to show that I was there and nothing more was said.''

"Did Mr. Carron sound angry?"

Alan pursed his lips. "Old Carron wasn't the man to utter
threats, but this sounded remarkably like one to me.''

He opened the door, went out and closed it behind him.
Finch was left to wonder if there hadn't been something faintly
spiteful about the young man's voice.

"D'you think that's true, Archie?" he asked.

"That it was his sister who wanted to live here, and that he
only came down to oblige? Of course not. Why, even the maid
sees through him, the lazy lay-about.''

"I meant the story about Mrs. Brooks quarrelling with her
uncle. We can't close our eyes to the possibility that Mr. Carron's
death may have had nothing to do with Tamara Lubova and the
Lake of Fire." He shook a ruminating head. "I think we'll
interview Istvan Kardos next. If it doesn't offer a solution, at
least it'll be an experience.''

Kardos came into the room as onto a stage. Indeed, it was
almost uncanny to see him, so exactly did he correspond to his
television image. His expression, his attitude, both had changed
to meet the changed circumstances. Yet the impact was the
same. It was, Finch decided, a matter of personality.

"Inspector!" The singer had halted halfway between door
and desk. He stood there, looking searchingly at the detective.
Some of his buoyancy had gone. He appeared tired, even distressed. Wilted was the word that came into Finch's mind. It was
almost as if he had just emerged from some ordeal. "You see in
me a most miserable and mistaken man. I act out of the best—
and disaster come of it. I try to save a life and one is taken. I put
up with the cold, the discomfort, the lack of service, the revoke,
the cooking—no, that is not bad. Miss Harkness expresses her
secret self in her cooking perhaps. It has élan. A dash of
recklessness. Yes, when I consider the cooking of Miss Harkness
I confess I am surprised.

"And for what do I suffer all this? I think now that my Tamara is dead and the diamond stolen. Why else was the old man killed? Shall Istvan Kardos then chase a thief? Never!" He drew himself up in an attitude of great nobility. "I have no more interest in this so uncomfortable a house. I ask only to be allowed to return to London."

Finch had watched, fascinated. It was the television programme all over again. "The laws of this country will not permit me to agree to your request," he said formally. Adding to himself, And don't tell me the news comes as any surprise. "I cannot allow anyone to leave this house until the enquiry is finished."

Kardos sighed heavily. "Then I stay. And I tell you, not what is in my heart—it is not the time for that. But what I have thought and done since I entered this house."

He sat down in the chair opposite the detective. He shot a quick cautious glance towards the closed door. He leaned across the table and his voice was no more than a whisper. A sibilant whisper. It would, Finch felt sure, have carried to the gallery or to the back row of the pit.

Kardos told him of his arrival at No. 9. Of his attempt to identify his one-time love. "For at that time, you understand, I think Tamara is here. I ask myself, is it the fat one? The black eyed one with the curious shape? The one in the chair who glare like crazy? How could I decide?" He described the playing of the gramophone record. "Next day I find that Madame Kosetti have many of my recordings but at the time I think it is a signal from Tamara."

Kardos went on to describe his night's vigil—waiting, he said, in the hope that she would make some further move. "For then, you must understand, I did not know that she was dead—or even that, if alive, she could only be Madame Kosetti."

He went on to draw a moving picture of himself as a man torn by indecision. Should he, or should he not, tell his story to Miss Harkness. "I take out my letter and then I see something I have not noticed before. I see that it has been steamed open and resealed. I knew then that only one course was open to me. I must tell all. I ask myself what will she do, this young lady. She cry perhaps? She faint? She send for the police? I prepare myself for anything."

"And what did she do?"

Kardos shook his head sadly. "She laugh. She refuse to

take me seriously. Ah, she has the responsibility, this hard one. Half an hour later and this man, Mr. Carron, is dead.''

Finch nodded. ''And you realised that your quest was ended. That Tamara Lubova must be dead too?''

Kardos sighed deeply. He had a fine chest expansion. ''I had suspected it earlier. The excellent Daisy tell me that a Madame Rakosi die here about three years ago.'' He raised a muscular hand and let it fall heavily onto the table top. ''I think she was Tamara. She still had the looks, the gaiety. Like me, she too was the foreigner.''

''And the diamond, the Lake of Fire?''

''I do not know where that is—but I tell you something.'' Again he glanced towards the closed door. Then he leaned still further across the table and his voice grated. ''Do not be deceived by Mr. Gadsby. I spend an hour, two hours with him. At first I think him of a simplicity unusual in a grown man. Then I become suspicious.'' The gold teeth gleamed but Mr. Kardos was not smiling. ''Very carefully I turn the conversation to the diamond. I ask the leading question and he fence with me. With great skill I question him. And I get nothing from him. Nothing at all but the platitude. It is not natural. So I say, Inspector, beware of the simple Mr. Gadsby. He deceive the household but he do not deceive me, Istvan Kardos. He has the diamond perhaps. Perhaps even he take the life of the so respectable solicitor when he let him in.''

''That's a very interesting theory,'' said Finch admiringly. ''I'll certainly watch him.''

''Then I retire. I leave all in your capable hands.'' Mr. Kardos rose to his feet. He bowed. He smiled. He managed to express his deep distress at his own part in the tragedy, his relinquishment of any participation in future enquiries and his boundless faith in the capabilities of the man before him. All at one and the same time.

It was a superb finale.

''The naughty old foreigner,'' said Finch staring after him. ''But at least we know where we stand with him. He means to go after that diamond come hell or high water.''

''I thought he was telling the truth except about this chap, Gadsby,'' said Slater. ''I couldn't make out what he was up to there.''

''And I thought he was telling the truth there. It was the rest I doubted.'' Finch lighted a cigarette and blew a cloud of smoke towards the ceiling, tipping his chair back until it balanced on two legs. "It was his insistence that only Madame Rakosi or Madame Kosetti could have been Tamara Lubova that betrayed his bad faith. He must know as well as I do that the Russians along with the Greeks have the ability to learn our language so well that they can pass as English." Adding significantly, "As this country found to its cost not so long ago."

Comprehension dawned on Slater's lantern-jawed face. "You mean that chap Lonsdale, in the Naval Spy Trial? Yes, of course. He turned out to be a Russian." And then, "But that would mean that perhaps Mrs. Winfield—oh no, I can't believe that."

"Why not?" said Finch airily, though he found it difficult to believe himself. "After all, the missionary zeal of the Reverend Charles Winfield may have had its effect. And I see from Enderby's notes (and he has so much local information at his finger tips that it's a pleasure to work with him) that Winfield was a padre in the First World War and so might well have found himself in Austria."

Magda Brooks was the next to be interviewed. She was dressed simply and expensively in black. She was pale and haggard under her careful make-up. She gripped an evening bag so convulsively that her knuckles showed white. Her smile was a purely social gesture.

Finch sprang up. He set a chair for her two inches from where it had been before. She was, he saw, the kind of woman who would respond best to V.I.P. treatment.

"I do apologise for having to question you at a time like this, but unfortunately I have no option."

"I quite understand." Again Magda smiled palely. "I'm afraid I behaved rather badly when I heard of Uncle Rupert's death. But this wasn't the first time. I seem marked out for tragedy."

Finch looked concerned. "I'm sorry to hear that."

"My first husband was killed in Korea. My second met with a terrible accident whilst working for Rand Reefs Consolidated. An avalanche of rock fell on him."

"Leaving you with no near relations?"

"I had no one but Uncle Rupert. That was why I came down here." Magda added fretfully, "And it was so unnecessary."

"In what way?"

"I begged him to come back to England but he wouldn't." It took Finch a moment to realise that she was speaking of her second husband. "He liked the life in South Africa. Oh, there was nothing wrong with it. I liked it myself but in London there was so much that I could have done for him. There Harry could have really counted for something.'' She spoke so bitterly that the echo of a hundred quarrels seemed to spring up in the room about them.

Finch wagged a mournful head. Perhaps Harry had not been the man for her. Or perhaps, like most men, he had preferred to run his own life.

''Had you been married long?''

''Two years.''

Finch murmured soothingly of shock. After a little he got her to talk of her life in Seamarsh. It sounded pleasant enough. She had friends. She had money. She had also made herself comfortable enough at No. 9 and had the good sense to recognise the fact.

''Not that there isn't something a little macabre about the place when one comes in late,'' Magda told Finch. ''That dreadful hall and nine times out of ten, one or other of the old ladies wandering about the corridors. They don't speak, just glide past one like *revenants*—except Madame Kosetti. Such a sight in an old sable coat and her hair done up in a sort of monstrous turban making her look at least eleven feet tall. She usually complains of insomnia, which isn't surprising since she sleeps most of the day. She complains of her heart too but that's all nonsense. Only the strongest organ would stand up to the treatment she gives it with her tantrums and hysterics.''

The conversation went on to the arrival of Istvan Kardos. ''Of course one couldn't help suspecting that someone in the house had written to him following his television broadcast,'' said Magda thoughtfully. ''Indeed, I went as far as to try and draw him out about it. He has the reputation of being rather a dangerous man to offend. Not at all the kind of person one would care to see in any sort of argument with one of the old ladies.''

She had intended to talk the situation over with her uncle, she told Finch, but events had moved too quickly for her. No, she had not known that he was coming to the house.

''He was a kind man and he was fond of Sara who, as you may have discovered, is a very nice person. He's got her out of a good many scrapes. Or, rather, he's got her out of the scrapes resulting from her brother's bad behaviour. Alan is utterly irresponsible about money and Sara is unwise enough to pay his debts for him over and over again. She's always threatening to cut off supplies but somehow he manages to talk her round."

"Does he have any success as an actor?"

"He would have—if he weren't so unreliable. If he sets off to an audition he gets no further than some girl friend. And when he does land a contract he's simply Hell on wheels. Already he's managed to get himself black-listed by half the managers and producers in London."

"Then how does he propose to live?"

Magda shrugged her plump shoulders. "He did think of a rich wife—even though she were nine years his senior."

"You?" Finch laughed with genuine amusement. "The conceited young so and so."

Magda smiled faintly. "He took my refusal awfully well. Only. . . ." She hesitated.

"Only what?"

Said Magda slowly, "Sometimes I've wondered whether he was really as big-hearted as he seemed. Whether he wasn't just waiting for the right moment to go gunning for me." A suspicion which Finch, recalling his interview with Alan Harkness, thought only too well grounded.

"One last thing. Have you any idea who might have killed your uncle?"

"None at all. It seems incredible—except on the grounds that he knew something about this diamond. And if that were the motive I can't help feeling that Mrs. McGee can be eliminated from your list of suspects. She is your true gambler. If she had had the diamond she would have pawned it long ago, having first convinced herself that she would soon be able to redeem it."

"That seems a very sound argument."

Again there came that expressive shrug. "Usually I'm a very sound woman."

"And you were on the best of terms with your uncle."

The hand on the bag tightened its grip a little. Beyond that Magda Brooks showed no sign of emotion. "I loved him very much," she said. "And he loved me." And that, Finch decided, was hardly an answer to his question but then Magda Brooks had struck him as an astute, strong-willed woman, not easily thrown off her balance. And that made even stranger her complete collapse on hearing of her uncle's murder.

There remained now only the enigmatic Mr. Gadsby to be interviewed.

Finch and Slater regarded him with great interest, if not as yet with suspicion. As Kardos had said, at first sight he appeared an altogether colourless man. A pale man with long pale hands. A mournful character, wearing a dark grey suit that gave him a vaguely clerical air.

When he came nearer they saw that he had on a really beautiful waistcoat of yellow watered silk. This, Finch considered, struck an incongruous note. It was, he felt, a definite deviation on a theme of insensibility.

Mr. Gadsby slumped into a chair. "What a terrible man," he said at once. "I was so thankful when you sent for him. Of course, one has heard that opera singers are inclined to be temperamental and easily upset but Mr. Kardos. . . ." He took out a handkerchief and wiped his face with it. "He talked and talked. I really began to think that he was demented. All about a diamond and a lady he'd been in love with years ago. I confess I couldn't make head nor tail of his story."

Finch stifled a desire to laugh. So much for Mr. Kardos and his great skill in questioning. In the simplest possible words Finch explained.

"Poor fellow! After all these years," said Mr. Gadsby at the end. "He must have loved her very much."

Finch felt a sudden sympathy with Kardos. Could Mr. Gadsby—could anyone—be as naïve as that? And with that waistcoat . . . ?

"I fancy that Mr. Kardos is more concerned for the whereabouts of the diamond," said Finch, "than the welfare of the lady."

"Indeed?" And then as the meaning of the detective's words sank in, "Good Heavens! I see what you mean."

"Mr. Kardos," Finch amplified, "was hoping that you could identify Tamara Lubova."

The pale hands fluttered ineffectually. The pale eyes slid past Finch. "I never heard of her until this evening."

"How long have you been here?"

"Seven years. I came two years before Mrs. Harkness' death." Mr. Gadsby had cheered up slightly. He seemed to think that Finch had changed the subject, as indeed he did the next moment, struck by a sudden suspicion.

"Mrs. Harkness died in her bed I trust?"

"Alas," said Mr. Gadsby sadly. "No. She was in collision with a lorry. At least, her car was in collision with a lorry. The chauffeur, Rogers—a good fellow—was killed instantaneously.

Mrs. Harkness died in the ambulance. Mrs. McGee, who was with her at the time, was barely scratched.''

"Indeed?" All kinds of ideas were chasing through Finch's mind. He tried some of them on Mr. Gadsby but the latter remained maddeningly, almost unbelievedly, non-committal. He gazed sadly at Finch. He tugged at his depressed looking moustache. Where it was possible he made haste to agree.

"I'm sure you're right there. . . . I couldn't agree more. . . . There's a lot in what you say. . . .''

When he got up to go Finch remarked, "That's a very fine waistcoat you're wearing, if I may say so.''

A faint gleam of emotion passed, like a watery sunrise, over Mr. Gadsby's face. "I was fortunate enough to inherit half a dozen of them from my father.'' His fingers slid over the material as if he were drawing music from it. "There is a lilac . . . But I think . . . Yes, I really think that this is my favourite.''

When he had gone, Finch, like Mr. Kardos, found in himself the seed of doubt. Could one be so negative, inoffensive and incurious as Mr. Gadsby? And then there was that waistcoat . . . just as much a thing of beauty as the Lake of Fire. . . .

He went along the passage to the office. He rang up the police station and spoke to Superintendent Enderby. "I suppose old Mrs. Harkness' death was purely accidental?''

"Certainly it was—except maybe in the sense that the lorry driver was drunk. Why?''

Said Finch softly, "Because the deaths of two other of the residents of No. 9 were not.''

Chapter 8

To Sara the hall at No. 9 now had the mysteriousness of an old battlefield. Haunted, not by the dead Tamara, but by the two people whom she had known.

Mrs. Winfield's whining voice complained from the shadows and the sound of her muffled feet crossed the perimeter of the hall just out of sight. Mr. McGee too was there. *She looks as if something had frightened her to death.* What else had he said? Their lost voices nagged at her mind like something shut out and trying to gain admittance.

She put down the tray and stood looking about her. She caught sight of her reflection in a hanging glass. She glanced at it idly at first and then with sudden interest. Her interview with the Inspector had done nothing for her looks. Her cheekbones seemed to stand out, sharp and white. There were blue smudges at the corners of her mouth. But, at least, she looked alive again. Human—even intelligent.

She turned to see Finch himself crossing the hall towards her. "So Miss Millamont is about to begin her diet of eggs," he commented. "And you seem to be allowing for every eventuality."

"I want her to have something," Sara excused the array. "I don't think she can be meaning to eat the eggs raw."

"I imagine she'll be satisfied once she's broken them and found them uncontaminated. D'you mind if I come up with you? I'd like to speak to Miss Millamont—and I could carry the tray."

"Thank you. Come if you like but I don't think she'll talk to you."

"I fancy I know what makes her tick." Finch picked up the tray.

"You seem rather a conceited man," said Sara severely.

90

"D'you know," said Finch in a surprised tone, "I've been told that before."

Since Sara refused to go up in the lift and Finch had examined it already, they agreed to go by way of the stairs.

On the first floor Kardos passed them. He was wrapped in a heavy black silk dressing gown and carried a bulging sponge bag conspicuously, like a stage property. He bowed and smiled. Sara thought again how essentially terrifying he was, in spite of being round and brown and merry looking, and pondered why.

There was no one about on the second floor. Indeed the house seemed to be quieter the higher they went. The silence on the attic floor was complete. So complete that it might have been a premonition of disaster and No. 9 fated to be bankrupt and deserted.

Sara turned to the right. "Miss Millamont's room is the only one that doesn't overlook the Square," she remarked. She paused in front of a door and knocked.

"It's me, Sara. I've brought you the eggs. Inspector Finch is with me. He wants to talk to you."

There came the sound of a bolt being drawn. The door opened a little and Miss Millamont poked her head out. She was still fully dressed.

"Thank you, Sara. How kind you are." She looked at Finch. "I'm afraid I have nothing to say to the police," she added loftily. "I was up here when the crime was committed and knew nothing about it until I heard the maid, Daisy, screaming."

"Well, the Inspector probably has something to say to you," said Sara rather tartly. "And, anyway, he'll want to put down the tray."

"Oh dear! Of course! I had forgotten the tray." Positive action of any sort threw Miss Millamont into a flutter. "Yes, do come in." She backed into her room as she spoke. "It's not very tidy I fear. And there is not very much space."

This last was an understatement. The room, comfortably if shabbily furnished, was cluttered wherever clutter was possible. Photographs in leather and tarnished silver frames, china ornaments, cut glass bottles, shell flowers, hand-painted potted meat jars and strips of brightly coloured silk were in profusion. The bed was littered with odd pieces of fur, buckram and wire.

"Now, where can you put the tray?" Miss Millamont looked about her helplessly, finger to her lip.

"The floor seems the only answer," said Finch. "I'll put it

down close to the gas ring.'' He noticed that the statuette of St.
Nicholas had not yet been returned to the mantelpiece.

"Thank you. How kind! My room isn't often as untidy as
this but you see, I was making myself a hat.'' Miss Millamont
added impressively, "A fur hat. A bit of *real* fur always looks
well I think.''

"Miss Millamont,'' said Sara, an expression of mild exasperation on her face, "we'll clear a couple of chairs and sit
down, while you do whatever you think with the eggs. You must
be starving.''

"If you're sure you won't think me rude?'' Miss Millamont
had been hovering rather feverishly over the tray. "Prolonged
abstention from food does tend to make one a little faint.''

"Yes, I'm awfully sorry about that. I did tell Daisy to bring
you up the eggs but I suppose she decided not to do it.''

Miss Millamont shook her head sadly. "Maids are so
provoking these days, are they not? I remember my uncle Charles
saying—he was the one in the Indian army—that really one
might just as well employ high caste Brahmins. He only came
back to England after the war and found the working classes
sadly changed.'' She had broken one of the eggs into a basin and
was studying it under the electric light. "He died only a few
years ago yet I don't think you ever met him, Sara?''

"No but from what I've heard of him, I'm sure I should
have liked him,'' said Sara kindly but untruthfully.

Miss Millamont broke a second and then a third egg. "One
can't be too careful,'' she murmured in a preoccupied manner.
"You have brought a frying pan? How thoughtful. And I have a
little butter. So if you really don't mind I'll make myself an
omelette.''

She bustled about, from a cupboard to the tray and back
again. She produced butter in a screw of paper, a rather stale-
looking end of a loaf, a little milk in a plastic cup.

"You could have tinned soup,'' said Finch suddenly. "The
thin sort, not the condensed. Or, indeed, any kind of liquid thin
enough to leak out if the tin is tampered with. Miss Harkness
might collect them in a suitcase at some shop—a different shop
each time.''

Miss Millamont stood stock still. "A different shop each
time?'' There was consternation in the faded blue eyes. "But
that sounds as if I shall be up here for weeks. You should be
ashamed of yourself, Inspector, for such a defeatist attitude.
Have you *no* idea who killed Mr. Carron?''

"How can I have," Finch retorted, "if no one will tell me what they know?"

"But the police, Inspector. I have never been brought in contact with the police. Except, of course, to enquire my way. And then, I must confess, I found them most helpful."

"You will be helping the cause of justice."

Miss Millamont pursed her lips. "Papa always said that a gentlewoman should do nothing to call attention to herself."

"But wouldn't your father have expected you to fulfil the duty you owe to your class and upbringing?"

Miss Millamont wavered. "But really, Inspector, I know nothing. The very idea that that Lubova woman is in the house seems to me to be ludicrous."

"Was in the house," Finch corrected. "It seems that she is dead and that someone else has the diamond."

"Someone has the Lake of Fire?" Miss Millamont's eyes grew round, whether with envy or surprise Finch could not decide.

"Then you've heard of the stone before today?"

"Oh yes—but it was a long time ago."

"Did you hear about it from someone in the house?"

"No one in the house ever tells me anything. Madame Kosetti confides in Mrs. McGee I believe. And Mrs. Bradshaw used to live in Mrs. Winfield's pocket but I have always been odd man out."

"Then Madame Rakosi never mentioned it?"

"Madame . . . ? Dear me, no. We scarcely exchanged half a dozen words all the time we were in the house together." Adding with an air of disapproval, "She was what I believe is known as a man's woman."

"Yet you went to her room shortly after she died."

Miss Millamont opened her eyes very wide. "I did no such thing, Inspector."

"Oh yes, you did," said Sara severely. "I was there when you opened the door. When you saw me you went away again."

"Oh that! I think you'll admit that I didn't actually go into the room."

"But what did you want?" Sara persisted.

"To say a prayer," answered Miss Millamont with an innocent air. "When I saw you there I concluded that that was your intention too so naturally I went away again." Adding piously, "One prays so much better alone and undistracted I always think."

Sara remained looking rather severe but Finch had difficulty in not laughing. "Then when was it you heard of Tamara Lubova and the diamond?"

"It was years ago. When I was governess to the Foeldis. I can remember Madame Foeldi returning to the house one evening in a terrible state. She had gone to a party in a private house and that brazen creature, as she called her, had actually been there. Not only that," Miss Millamont's voice dropped impressively, "she was wearing the Lake of Fire around her neck as a pendant. It was said that the Emperor was furious about the affair and set the secret police on her to recover the diamond."

"What happened to the archduke?"

"He was killed in the war."

Finch raised his eyebrows. "And, with her protector dead and the secret police at her heels, Tamara Lubova managed to keep the diamond? She must have been a very resourceful and clever young woman."

"Did you ever see her?" Sara asked.

Miss Millamont nodded. "Indeed yes. I can remember seeing her once or twice riding in her carriage. A very pretty woman." She poured the beaten egg into the frying pan. Then she added seriously, "I think—mind you I'm not sure. But I *think* her nose turned up at the tip."

At this Sara burst out laughing.

"Miss Millamont," said Finch, "in those few words you have done more to recreate Tamara Lubova than pages of official description."

"If I should recall anything more of value," promised Miss Millamont graciously, "I will come direct to you. So much more satisfactory, I always think, to go to the highest authority."

And since the omelette was now cooked, Sara and the Inspector left her to eat it.

They retraced their steps. Past the head of the stairs. Past rooms full of shadows and criss-crossed with moonlight. Giving glimpses of incongruous lumber. A dressmaker's dummy in wire like an articulated skeleton. Hats and odd bits of finery. A garden figure in lead of a faun. Piles of old magazines and large leather trunks with curved lids, stuck with scraps of foreign labels. A bird's cage with a stuffed parrot caught in the shaft of light from the door, dusty but with its eyes glinting in a travesty of intelligent scrutiny.

"They give a rather sinister illusion of life," Finch murmured in his soft voice. "Rather like the Chamber of Horrors at

Madame Tussaud's. Or the opening shots of a French film. One feels that they must have significance of one sort or another.''

There was a light under Madame Kosetti's door and a slight rustling movement came from within. Sara knocked. The sound ceased and so tense a silence followed that to the girl at least there came an uncomfortable impression of its occupant holding her breath behind the closed door.

"Come!" cried Madame Kosetti's wheezing voice.

Sara opened the door. She paused in surprise. She had expected to find only the one person in it. Instead all three old women were there, sitting in silence with still, expressionless faces.

From over Sara's shoulder Finch looked into the room. He saw that it was long and low and cluttered like a junk shop. Piles of old newspapers littered the floor. It had the close smell of ancient sachets, dust and drugs. Out of a pool of varying shadows the bed rose mounded in immense curves to where, propped up on half a dozen pillows, Madame Kosetti lay on a moth-eaten sable coat worn as a bed jacket.

Finch soon found that Superintendent Enderby had been right. The three old ladies had predetermined their attitude and their answers. They had, they assured him, been all together as now when Mr. Carron had been murdered. They too, like Mrs. Brooks, had not known that the old solicitor was in the house until they had gone downstairs on hearing Daisy's screams.

Mrs. McGee admitted to having seen Kardos' television appearance by chance in a shop window in the town. Having heard his voice so often on gramophone records, she had been interested enough to stop her chair and watch. On her return she had recounted what she had heard to Madame Kosetti and Mrs. Bradshaw. Miss Millamont had known nothing of the programme until that morning.

Mrs. McGee ended with a harsh laugh, "It was a romantic tale. I thought it would strike a kindred chord in Vera Millamont's maidenly breast."

"You destroyed her imaginary life," said Sara indignantly. "It was most unkind."

Madame Kosetti gave a guttural chuckle. "The English Miss in the house of the bourgeois banker of Vienna."

"I consider that she behaved very bravely," said Sara.

"You English are like that," Madame Kosetti declared in a spiteful voice. "Soft, vacillating. But at the last willing to die for your convictions."

"And not a bad thing either," said Sara hotly.

Madame Kosetti closed her eyes. "Bad, bad?" she said fretfully. "Who said anything about its being bad? It is worse than bad. It is misleading."

Finch had taken no part in this conversation. He was watching Mrs. Bradshaw with fascinated interest. She was engaged in removing a couple of inches from the hem of her skirt. Raising her small black lace-up boots into the air she would pass the ball of wool from one hand to another beneath her legs with every complete circle. Her face, he noticed, had turned an alarming shade of purple. As no one else paid any attention to her singular behaviour he decided that it must be a commonplace occupation.

Reluctantly he withdrew his gaze. "But we didn't come here to talk about Miss Millamont, except to remark that she seems to be the odd one out. Why is that?"

"She is silly—and she steals. Yes, she does, Sara," Mrs. McGee insisted. "She is like a jackdaw. Let her into your room and something will vanish."

"And Mr. Gadsby? He too seems on his own."

"That is not our doing." Madame Kosetti's great moon face twisted into a mask of contemptuous amusement. "He is afraid of life. Of women—even such women as we have become."

"I remember my late husband saying that Mr. Gadsby's father was a bibliomaniac and squandered a fortune on his hobby," said Mrs. McGee. "He lived in a strange world of unreality and, no doubt, taught his son to do the same."

"Of beautiful unreality," amended Madame Kosetti.

"And do Tamara Lubova and the Lake of Fire enter into any of this?"

"We know nothing of either," said Madame Kosetti firmly, "although both must have had their beauty."

"And both were in this house?" Finch noticed that Mrs. McGee looked frightened as well as unhappy. He wondered whether she was going to prove the weak link in the chain of disavowals.

"Can the Inspector be suggesting that I am a whore from the streets of Vienna? Surely not," said Mrs. Bradshaw in the muffled tones necessitated by her position.

"I'm not looking for her among you at all," said Finch, "for I believe her to be dead."

"Come, Gordon," said Mrs. Bradshaw. "That's better. The officer was withdrawn his offensive remark. We can afford to overlook the insinuation."

"But I still want to identify this woman," said Finch.

"We know nothing of her. Nor of the Lake of Fire," said Madame Kosetti again. She added in a sing-song voice, "Nothing but nothing."

"We had decided, Gordon, had we not, that that would be the best thing to say," said Mrs. Bradshaw. "Or, if not the best, then, at least, the safest."

"You will only be safe when the murderer is caught," said Finch. And saw, from their expressions, that something more than mere physical safety was involved.

He decided on shock tactics. "I must ask you to think very carefully about this; for it seems probable that it is not the first murder in the house. But that Mrs. Winfield and also Mr. McGee were murdered."

"That also we have considered," said Madame Kosetti. And discounted, said her tone of voice. "Not beforehand you understand but only since we heard of the death of Mr. Carron."

Mrs. McGee said nothing. But two tears ran down her hard red cheeks. Finch turned to her, "If you know nothing of the diamond, what is it that has wrecked your peace of mind?" he asked her.

Mrs. McGee put her handkerchief to her eyes. It was a large white handkerchief which obscured most of her face. "It was the money," she muttered into it. "The money my husband left. When he died I reinvested it in the very shares he'd warned me against. I lost it all. Timothy would hardly rest quiet in his grave if he knew."

"Oh come, Mrs. McGee, that was sheer bad luck, wasn't it? After all, you might just as easily have made a fortune."

Mrs. McGee removed the handkerchief. "That's what I always say, Inspector," she said eagerly. "It was sheer bad luck. Even now if I could raise a little capital . . ."

"You'd lose it as quickly as you lost the rest," interrupted Madame Kosetti, with a malignant glance at Finch. A glance that tacitly admitted that she had been out-manoeuvred.

Finch did not speak again, just sat looking curiously at Mrs. McGee.

Mrs. McGee spoke suddenly as if the silence preyed on her courage. "I heard someone up here last night. Just footsteps passing my door."

Finch stirred. "What time was this?" So I was right, he thought. She is the weakest link.

"I don't know," Mrs. McGee looked acutely uncomfortable. She avoided catching anyone's eyes as she spoke. "I woke up and couldn't go to sleep again. I lay awake for hours. That's how I came to hear the footsteps."

"If you were awake for hours, you must have heard the church clock striking," said Sara.

"Oh yes. Now you mention it I believe I did hear the clock," said Mrs. McGee weakly. "It was just after three o'clock."

"Did you recognise the footsteps?"

Mrs. McGee shook her head.

"I understand that you four ladies sleeping up here are often about at night. Couldn't it have been one of you?"

"It wasn't one of us. These footsteps tiptoed past." Mrs. McGee looked both frightened and obstinate. "Why should we do that?"

"And that's all you heard? Just someone going straight down the passage." He was thinking that if it had been Mr. Kardos he would have paused to look in at each open door.

Mrs. McGee shook her head. "Whoever it was came back again about ten minutes later," she muttered.

Finch glanced at Sara. "Any idea where this unidentified person might have been going?"

"There are several rooms but I suppose the most likely would have been the lumber room," said Sara brightly.

Finch's eyebrows climbed. "What lumber is in it?"

"Mostly old Mrs. Harkness' things." Sara saw that she had made things worse by her prevarication. That, by it, she had called attention to the ambiguous shadow of her brother. "The letters and housekeeping books you wanted are there."

"Or they were there," said Madame Kosetti with another of her wide protracted smiles.

"It won't matter their having gone," said Sara hotly, "if you'd tell the Inspector what you know about Tamara Lubova."

Madame Kosetti's smile grew a little fixed. "So you too want us to take the long journey into the past? But to what end?" she asked ironically. "We live in a ghost world. Peopled with those who are long dead. Pleasures that are past. Loves that are cold."

Mrs. McGee was staring straight in front of her, drumming nervously with her fingers on the arm of her chair. "We know nothing that would help. Why do you bother us?"

"We shall discover the identity of Tamara Lubova in time," Finch warned them.

"Time to us has become only a series of reflections in a dusty mirror." Madame Kosetti's great yellowish face was still. She seemed to brood over the remark with the air of a connoisseur.

Mrs. Bradshaw rose suddenly to her feet. She shook out her skirt and peered down at the effect. "It's gravity that does it," she announced. "The law of gravity—pulling, pulling. You can't get round it, knit how you will."

One after another they had seized on their cues. Yet, behind their words, Finch could sense an atmosphere of apprehension and dismay. They had made their choice but fear of death and not the night temperature chilled the air. Madame Kosetti's relentless smile had become positively macabre.

He carried away a picture of the overcrowded room and the three old faces watchful and staring in the shadows.

Chapter 9

To Sara the night seemed full of threats. "If only morning would come," she thought anxiously. She went into the kitchen. It was empty but she saw that Daisy had stayed on and done all the work. All that is but filling the two hods with coal for the sitting-room grate. They stood there, black, empty, mute symbols of the maid's sour conviction that to fill them should be Alan's work.

So there was only that to do, then she could go to bed. Sara picked them up, walked along the passage and kicked open the door which led to the cellar steps.

At once she became aware that there was a light below. Sounds came to her ears. Small hollow sounds as if someone were moving about the rooms beneath.

She let the door swing silently together behind her. Crept forward on tiptoe, one step at a time, holding her breath. Now the sounds became definite. She had no difficulty in recognising them. Someone was raking out the boiler.

Alan, she thought. It must be Alan. Then the improbability of this struck her. She hurried forward and peered into the boiler room.

Sergeant Slater was there, squatting down on his haunches. The door of the boiler was open and the glow from within cast a ruddy glow over his lantern-jawed face. He turned his head, looking round enquiringly as she appeared.

A small cardboard box stood nearby and a pile of charred and half-burned paper lay on the floor.

Sara went forward swiftly. "Why are you burning those?" she asked. "They must be. . . ." She broke off.

"Old Mrs. Harkness' papers and housekeeping books." Slater spoke lightly. "And I'm not burning them. I'm rescuing them."

"So someone did take them last night from the room in the attics?"

"Yes, I couldn't find them there so I thought I'd look for them here." Slater poked at the charred pile with a finger. "Letters, account books, invitations even. Trouble is, if the robbery took place last night, as seems likely, the thief has had plenty of time to examine his haul. And as it has since become red hot, no doubt the interesting ones, if any, have been removed and then more thoroughly destroyed than this lot."

He picked up the cardboard box, tapped the bottom to empty it of bits, and then remarked, "I borrowed this from the larder. It had some onions in it. I hope you don't mind?"

"Of course not." Sara spoke automatically. She wished that she could banish Alan and his possible complicity in the theft of the letters from her mind. It seemed to her that by the very acuteness of her mental discomfort she must communicate his name to her companion.

"Who made up the boiler tonight?"

There, it was done, she thought despairingly. "My brother I expect." She was proud to hear her voice so unconcerned. She added, "But that's not going to be much help to you. He wouldn't have taken the least interest in what he was doing, just opened the top and poured in the coke."

"Does he always make up the boiler?"

"He's been doing it recently." No need to say how recently. "But household chores aren't really in his line. He means well but half the time he doesn't even remember to rake the boiler out."

There was silence for a moment. It seemed to curl between them like a question.

"Of course, anyone could have dropped them in," said Slater casually. He had the easy stance of the physically fit as he stood, not looking at her, but at the box in his hand.

"What will you do with the burnt remains?" asked Sara with an equal assumption of unconcern.

"Leave them with Baker, the chap in the hall," said Slater. "Send them to the lab later." He smiled cheerfully at Sara. "I'll just tie up the box. Then there's something I want to show you upstairs."

Sara remembered the scuttles abandoned at the head of the stairs. "While you're doing that I'll just get the two coal scuttles and fill them."

Slater frowned. "Where are they?" he asked. "I'll fill

them.'' He went off. In a minute he was back. "What goes in them?"

"Coal for the sitting room. I'll show you." Sara led the way.

"Why doesn't your brother do this?"

"Because of his job. He has to consider his hands."

Slater opened his mouth to say something. Then closed it again. When he had filled the scuttles he said mildly, "Couldn't Daisy do it?"

"I couldn't ask her. She does so much already and none of it really her work. You see her real job was just to wait on Mrs. Harkness. Look after her clothes and do the sewing." Sara added, "I never met either my cousin or his wife but I seem to know them quite well, simply from hearing Daisy talk about them. And anyway," she added smiling, "she's usually out at this time. She has a bicycle and goes to her chapel. Sometimes she isn't back until the small hours of the morning."

"She's there now I think. At least, she isn't in the house." Slater led the way from the cellar, carrying the two full hods with effortless ease.

They came to the kitchen. There they halted as if by mutual consent. A comfortable comradeship seemed to have been established between them.

"I went down there once with my brother two years ago," said Sara. "To the chapel I mean. All through narrow back roads and little alley ways to a dark grimy looking building with a glass dome which was once the town's aquarium. The inside simply bursts on you. Colour and candles and incense. All sombre magnificence. Mr. Jolly had been brought up on the Book of Revelations. He'd worked it out that the world would end on January 18th. He didn't know which year, only the day. Such presumption—but it does upset poor old Daisy."

Slater, watching her, saw the planes of her face begin to melt into amusement. "Some sect, in some part of the world, is always expecting the world to end. It gives a needed bit of drama to otherwise drab lives," he remarked.

"That's all right for Daisy," Sara agreed, "but how about Mr. Gadsby? He's one of them too. I would never have known but he was there that day." She added, after a moment's reflection, "Only quite a different Mr. Gadsby, I scarcely recognised him. He was so enthusiastic. Took us everywhere, even out onto the roof by a little door opening from the gallery. We had to see and admire everything—except some plaster figures. He loathed them."

"That's odd," said Slater slowly. "When the chief asked him about it he was as vague as over everything else."

"How extraordinary! I've always remembered him as he was then. It made me feel that there was a second Mr. Gadsby hidden somewhere inside the first."

Slater frowned. "It's a queer thing but no one in this house is quite what they seem."

"If it comes to that," said Sara, who had an obscure feeling that she had somehow betrayed Mr. Gadsby, "your Inspector isn't quite what he seems either. Why, this evening, in the dining room he seemed positively to be enjoying himself."

"He doesn't enjoy murders," said Slater tolerantly. "He just enjoys solving them."

They left the kitchen, strolling towards the hall.

"Nice place for playing cops and robbers," Slater remarked conversationally.

"I never thought so until tonight." Sara's voice was low. "Now, everything seems changed. To have become a—a weapon in the hands of fear. The passage because one's footsteps echo. Honestly can you swear that there are only us two walking down it? The furniture because it's so big. Big enough to hide a murderer. The hall because the light's so poor. The lift . . ." She hesitated.

"Because old Mrs. Winfield died in it?"

"Actually I avoided the lift before that. You see, the old ladies use it as a sort of hide. Then if you go to use it, it suddenly sets off and leaves you stranded and staring after it. And if it's at the top floor and you bring it down it's quite possible that when you go to step in Mrs. Bradshaw will step out." Sara's expression was a mixture of wry amusement and exasperation. "I can never decide whether she spends hours actually in it waiting for it to be brought down. Or whether she has some method of her own and manages to hurl herself in it as it begins to move."

Slater chuckled. "Perhaps she comes down the shaft like a fireman," he suggested idly.

Sara looked at him quickly. "I once had a horrible dream about that," she confided. "Only it was Mrs. McGee who came down the shaft—as I ran down the stairs to get away from her. Only, of course, I couldn't get away. She came flapping after me across the hall and her legs had turned into a tail like a mermaid. I was terrified."

Slater looked at her compassionately. Always tearing herself to pieces over something, even in her sleep, he thought. He gave the cardboard box into Baker's care and followed Sara up the stairs.

On the first floor the silence was broken by the sound of Magda running the bath water. Mr. Gadsby appeared suddenly crossing the end of the passage. Sara reflected how often he had seemed to appear fleetingly like that since Mr. Carron's death, but she did not mention it to Slater.

Mr. Kardos' bedroom door was not quite shut. They could hear him humming cheerfully to himself. They went on up the second flight, aware that the humming had ceased, leaving behind it an uneasy picture of the little brown man standing behind his open door, listening to them pass.

On the second floor, Slater turned to the left, switching on the lights as if he knew his way about the house. He opened one of the bedroom doors.

"But no one uses this room," said Sara puzzled. She followed him to the far side of the old-fashioned brass bedstead. She gave an exclamation of dismay.

The statuette of St. Nicholas lay on the floor, smashed to fragments.

Sara looked at it with scared eyes. "Then Miss Millamont was speaking the truth. Someone did take it from her room last night."

Again the unspoken question curled between them. Alan? Had he slipped into Miss Millamont's bedroom during the night?

"But why . . . ?" Sara asked whispering.

"It was plaster," Slater explained. He saw that her face had tightened again into its customary fine drawn angles and hollows. "Someone thought the Lake of Fire might be embedded in it." He added reflectively, "Someone who hadn't given the matter much thought, since the whole point of owning the diamond is to have it somewhere handy so that one can gloat."

The door, opening suddenly, made them start. Daisy, still in her coat and hat, stood there. "I heard voices and I wondered who it was at this time of night. You ought to be in bed, miss." Adding sourly, "You'll find tomorrow's a day same as any other." She vanished as suddenly as she had appeared.

"I suppose she's right," said Sara slowly. Only she had a feeling that tomorrow was going to be even worse than today. "I had better go to bed."

Slater nodded. "You know this may be quite extraneous to the murder. We may never know who took the papers from the

attic nor who smashed Miss Millamont's St. Nicholas. May
never even need to know.''

They left the room.

"Is Daisy a night wanderer too?"

"Thank Heavens, no." Sara smiled. "Poor Daisy, she goes
through all these agonies every January. She's only missed one
Revelation Day since she's been here and that was when old
Mrs. Harkness died and she was away ill. Not that she minded
so much about Revelation Day—that could have been the same
anywhere. It was missing my cousin's funeral that upset her."

"Where does Daisy sleep?"

"On this floor. So do I and my brother and Mr. Gadsby.
Mr. Kardos and Mrs. Brooks are on the floor below. The four
old ladies," Sara nodded towards the attic stairs, "are up there. I
don't suppose they'll be out tonight."

Slater's smile broadened into a grin. "Don't you?" He
drew her silently towards the banisters.

Madame Kosetti had appeared in the hall far below. She
wore the sable coat over her nightdress and her great coils of hair
were encased in a turban-like silk square. She crossed to the lift,
ignoring the police constable, beating time with one hand and
singing an aria from "Traviata." In the other hand she held a
full glass of milk.

The singing dropped to a murmur partially drowned by the
whining of the old lift. It came to a halt and Madame Kosetti
stepped out. She looked momentarily taken aback at seeing Sara.
Then her face settled into a dolorous mask. Suffering flowed like
an incoming tide over her vast slab of a face.

"I could not sleep. My mind boiled in turmoil," she told
Sara mournfully. "I have been subjected to a cruel inquisition—
so I thought a little hot milk might settle the nerves. It is not
much." Her eyes strayed to Slater. She drew herself up to her
full height. "Torturer," she hissed. "Gestapo. Assassin!"

She swept past them and was out of sight before either of
them had recovered from the suddenness of her attack.

The local police, under Superintendent Enderby, had searched
Mr. Carron's house. Now they were doing the same for his
office. They had the assistance of Mr. Bell, managing clerk to
the firm of Harkness & Carron, and successor to the late Gordon
Bradshaw. He was a small, dried up little man but very businesslike. He had refused Enderby's suggestion that he should go
home to bed and looked pale and shocked.

Septimus Finch had joined the search party at the office some half an hour previously. Since then he had contrived to get on the Superintendent's nerves. He had refused to be interested in what went on. He had wandered aimlessly about, watching proceedings with a melancholy eye.

Now he sat in the swivel chair behind Mr. Carron's desk, twisting it gently from side to side.

Enderby came on the document relating to the mortgage of No. 9. He slapped it down on the desk, "Perhaps you'd care to look at that."

Finch looked up at him, surprised at his tone. He read the terms on which the mortgage had been given. The amount surprised him. "Seems a good sum to lend on such a property."

"I ventured to point that out at the time," said Mr. Bell in his clipped precise voice. "Mr. Carron said that Miss Harkness needed the money and that was the only way he could get her to accept it."

Finch's eyebrows climbed. "Needed it, did she? D'you happen to know what for?"

Mr. Bell pursed his thin lips. "I suppose, under the circumstances, there is no harm in my telling you. It was to keep her brother out of prison."

"What?" Enderby swung round, staring.

"Yes, indeed. The affair might very well have ended as a police matter. It appears that Alan Harkness and a couple of lazy young rascals were lent a flat in London by a friend, an actor, who was going to Australia with a touring company. They took the opportunity to work a flat-letting racket. Accepted a premium from a number of persons and then simply vanished with the money. Unfortunately for Mr. Harkness one of their victims recognised him in a film part. Traced him and would have prosecuted if it had not been for Miss Harkness. She managed to convince him—and herself too no doubt—that her brother had been led astray by his friends. She insisted on repaying all the people who had been swindled. Hence the size of the mortgage on No. 9."

"And none of them were prepared to prosecute?" Enderby sounded outraged. What really annoyed him was that this was something he should have known and had not done so.

"It was a case of either revenge or money," Finch pointed out. "They couldn't have both."

Mr. Bell nodded his neat head. "There was that aspect of the affair," he admitted.

Finch looked pensive. "So our Master Alan is something more than just lazy," he mused.

"And our Inspector interested in something at last," said Enderby.

Finch's eyebrows climbed still higher. "Do I give that impression? I'm worried, you know. Worried because there's something about this business I haven't grasped. There's Mrs. McGee and her gambling. She doesn't really regret it."

"Indeed?"

"And those three old ladies. They were frightened all right—frightened as Hell—yet they wouldn't tell me which of the household had been Tamara Lubova. Why?" His soft voice trailed away.

"Why is it so important to identify that woman?" Enderby thought that No. 9 should have been searched for the diamond.

"Mr. Carron only knew her identity and it was enough to get him murdered which suggests that the name of one will point to the other."

"As how?" Enderby asked cautiously.

"As Madame Rakosi and Mrs. Winfield. Mrs. Harkness and Mrs. McGee—or Daisy. Or Mrs. Winfield and Mrs. Bradshaw. Or indeed any suitable combination. You know! Going together—like ham and eggs."

The Superintendent walked away. Police work was police work and all laid down in the manual but the Scotland Yard man seemed to think it could be worked out by some crazy system of his own.

Behind him he heard Finch's voice raised again and Bell's voice in answer.

"You must have seen quite a lot of Mrs. Brooks. What did you think of her?"

"She was very self-reliant. Good at business too. She understood the stock market as well as any man. But I thought her hard and—well, arrogant. Any kind of failure was anathema to her."

"And she had such failures?"

"One, Inspector. Her second marriage. I hope you won't think I spied on her in any way. But going in and out of the room when she was here—and often at Mr. Carron's private residence when he was unwell—I couldn't help but overhear scraps of conversation."

"Well?"

"From what I overheard—and I may be wrong—it seemed

that Mrs. Brooks had been, in some way, responsible for her husband's death.''

"I heard that she and Mr. Carron had been quarrelling quite recently?''

Superintendent Enderby had returned, drawn by his interest in what was being said.

"I believe that to be a fact. Indeed I heard something of it not long ago. Last Monday week to be precise." Finch nodded. Precision seemed to be Mr. Bell's strong point. "I was just entering this room when I heard Mr. Carron cry out as if she had provoked him beyond endurance. ''Do you really believe that Harry will stay quietly where you put him—in his grave? Or that I'll be a party to such a thing indefinitely?''

"What did Mrs. Brooks say to that?''

"Nothing. Just swept out of the room without a glance at me—but she looked dreadful. And when I came in here Mr. Carron was sitting at his desk where you are now, with such an odd sort of expression on his face. A sort of startled look—as if he had said something that had been in his mind for a long time but which he'd never thought to hear himself say.''

There followed a silence. Enderby broke it. "But damn it, man!" he exploded. "Where does that lead us?''

"Up a particularly intriguing garden path,'' said Finch in his small voice.

The search went on without success. It began to look as if any knowledge Mr. Carron had had of Tamara Lubova had been carried in his head. Unless, as Finch pointed out, he had had some written evidence on him at the time of his death, in which case his murderer would have removed it.

Archie Slater arrived carrying the cardboard box. He looked cold and his coat was beaded with moisture. "The fog's pretty thick, sir,'' he told Finch. "I was thankful I hadn't far to come.''

"Any luck?'' Finch asked.

"No, sir. Whoever was up in the attic last night must have searched those trunks. I found what was left of Mrs. Harkness' papers stuffed into the boiler. They're pretty badly burned.''

Finch regarded the charred remains pensively. "Young Alan, I suppose.''

"I fancy his sister thought so,'' Slater admitted. He repeated his conversation with Sara. He had a good memory and Finch liked to know exactly what was going on.

Finch was most interested in her meeting with Mr. Gadsby

at the Chapel of the Watchful People. "So Mr. Gadsby does have another side to his nature," he commented. "What one might call the silk waistcoat side. He *is* capable of enthusiasm."

"He's capable of affection too," Enderby grunted. "When he first went to live at No. 9 he had a bull terrier called Ajax if I remember rightly. It became bad tempered in its old age. Used to sit on the doorstep showing its teeth. Bit one or two people. Finally it became a choice between leaving the house and putting the dog to sleep. Mr. Gadsby chose to leave. Went right out to the wilds where presumably there weren't any people to bite. Somewhere in the Highlands. Sutherland I believe."

"I remember that," said Mr. Bell. "It was only after the dog died that he wrote to Miss Harkness and asked to have his old room back."

Finch seemed very interested in this. More than, in Enderby's opinion, it warranted. "Mr. Gadsby never mentioned that he'd been away. Before this conversation I should have put that down to his being a man who found it impossible to communicate with his fellow men. Now I'm not so sure."

Chapter 10

Miss Millamont had long ago finished making her fur hat. She sat, the result unnoticed beside her, on the edge of her bed. She had been sitting there for some time. Terror welled up in her throat. Her heart thudded and icy fingers chilled her spine. It was, she thought shivering, the Vienna tenement all over again.

She was not in the least reassured by the sounds of footsteps passing at intervals. That they paused each time outside her door so that she could have called out had she so wished did not comfort her. "A policeman," she reflected automatically. "A policeman in the house. How common!" And her thoughts would go back to her immediate problem and the necessity to make a move.

The footsteps passed again. Miss Millamont glanced at the luminous face of the little travelling clock which stood by her bed. If she went now—and hurried—she would be back before the policeman's return.

Silently she slipped from the room. Silently drew the door to behind her. She could hear the man's footfalls retreating down the passage as he went on his round. She crept after him. Went down the narrow stairs away from him. How fortunate that she knew exactly where to tread to avoid those sudden and disconcerting cracks so easily produced from old wood.

She came to the second floor. Stood there for a moment listening. Aware of great patches of darkness in front of her. Aware, too, of her own loneliness. She might have been the last person alive in a world that had ceased to function. The last person but one—and that one a murderer. At the thought her veins seemed to run with ice and every sense to be raised to an abnormal, an almost painful, state of vigilance.

She turned to the right, forcing herself to go on. Here a window opened onto the Square. The light from a street lamp should have been shining in like a vision of normality. But not tonight. Tonight the window was a mirror backed by fog and her own reflection stared back helplessly at her as she passed.

There was no sound on the first floor. Mr. Kardos? Probably asleep. Mrs. Brooks? Miss Millamont's lips thinned. A selfish woman living only for herself.

She went on, pausing at the head of the last flight. Staring down into the darkness of the flagged passage. Only when she had satisfied herself that there was no one there did she continue down the stairs.

With great caution she pushed open the office door and stood looking into a pool of darkness that gradually resolved into separate pieces of furniture, as the silence resolved itself into a medley of small stirrings and whisperings that had nothing of the human about them.

She pushed the door to behind her. Stole across the floor and lifted the telephone receiver, waiting for the operator to answer. Suddenly she thought she heard a faint but definite sound behind her. She could not bring herself to turn. "Who's there?" she whispered.

She waited frozen with fear. Turning at last she saw that no one was in the room. *Outside the door then?* She listened and met with such utter and deadly silence that her heart seemed to die in her breast.

"Number please?" said the bored voice of the operator in her ear.

Miss Millamont put her lips right up to the receiver. "I want the police station please. And hurry. It's a matter of life and death." She kept her eyes fixed on the door, while her mind grew confused and she babbled. "A matter of life and death. A matter. . . ." And still no one burst in on her.

She waited. Aeons of time seemed to pass. At last she was through. She asked for Inspector Finch. She was told that he was not there but that a message could be given to him.

Not there! Miss Millamont was crushed with disappointment. "The highest authority," she thought frantically. "So much more satisfactory"—and did not know that she had spoken aloud.

"Who's that speaking?" asked the voice from the other end. "I didn't quite catch . . ."

"The message is for Inspector Finch. I want you to tell him that it's about the diamond. One does not gossip, you understand. I saw it arrive but I didn't realize the true meaning until just now."

The mention of the diamond—any diamond—was enough to galvanize the local police—"What's that, ma'am? I don't quite understand. If you'd explain . . . Hullo? Hullo? . . ."

But Miss Millamont, her mission, as she thought, accomplished, had replaced the receiver.

She crossed the floor towards the door. The silence seemed more intense than ever. She waited, until gradually it was borne in on her that no one was there. She opened the door and stood listening. To what? Her heart thudding? Her breath coming in unsteady gasps? There was no other sound.

She made her way to the foot of the stairs. The light was on in the passage above. She stared upwards shuddering. There was no sound. No one. Nothing. Only the bright empty mouth of the passage that might at any moment be blocked by . . .

Gasping she mounted the stairs. The first flight. The second. . . . Had there been a sound of footsteps somewhere behind her, faint as the vanishing remembrance of a dream?

Turning she fancied that she saw a shadowy figure, moving out of sight, round the far corner—Mr. Kardos.

She gave the smallest of cries. Picking up her dressing gown skirts she stumbled and raced up the remaining stairs. She slipped along the passage and into her own room.

Silently, swiftly, she closed the door. Shot the bolt. Switched on the light. I've done it, she thought triumphantly. I've done it and I'm safely back.

She was conscious of a great weariness. So cold too that she felt she would never be warm again. She turned out the light and stumbled towards the bed.

The search of Mr. Carron's office had proved fruitless. There was nothing that bore on the far past of any of the inhabitants of No. 9. Wearily Enderby signalled to Mr. Bell that the black tin boxes which littered the floor could be replaced.

"Six hours' work on my part and we're no further on," he grumbled. He glanced at the clock. The time was twelve minutes past two. "We may as well . . ." He broke off as the telephone rang. "What the devil . . . ?"

"You're probably right there." Finch picked up the receiver. He gave his name.

It was the sergeant in charge at the head police station. He gave Finch Miss Millamont's message. "She was confused and agitated but as soon as she mentioned the diamond the constable wrote down what she was saying word for word. From her voice it was an old lady speaking, he says. . . ."

"I know who it was. Now listen. I want you to ring No. 9. . . ."

"Beg pardon, sir," the sergeant interrupted, "but not knowing how long I'd be getting in touch with you I told the constable to do that very thing. He's still trying but the line seems to be dead. Maybe the receiver's off."

"Didn't the old lady replace it?"

"Yes, sir. She did. Looks as if someone's taken it off again—or cut the line."

Someone? The murderer? The thought slid into Finch's mind, chilling it. "Get round to No. 9 as quick as you can," he said. "I'll do the same from here."

Finch snapped the receiver back into place. His face was grim, a little pale. "Come on!" he said. He seized his coat and hat, struggling into them as he made for the door. He repeated what he had just been told.

"Miss Millamont, of course," he said. "And the murderer salvaging an extra ten minutes by isolating the house." He tore open the outer door. Paused in fresh dismay as the sea mist eddied around and the waiting police car loomed at him suddenly like some mirage of reality in a desert of nothingness.

"It's still quicker this way," Enderby declared, wrenching open the car door. They piled in. The Superintendent, Finch, Slater and a Sergeant Protheroe who had followed uninvited and now sprang smartly into the seat beside the driver.

"But why didn't Miss Millamont give her message to Pierce, the man patrolling those top two floors?" asked Enderby, subsiding onto the back seat and breathing heavily. "That's what I don't understand."

"She told us that," said Finch. He was sitting on the very edge of the seat, staring stonily into the fog. "She believed in going to the highest authority. And, in her screwy mind, that was me."

He had a sudden agonised vision of Miss Millamont in all the finery of her bits and pieces, creeping down the stairs, trembling, starting at each shadow—just as she must have crept down the tenement stairs in search of her missing charge so many years ago.

"And I boasted that I knew what made her tick," he muttered. "I knew but I never thought she'd . . . But that isn't any excuse. I should have thought."

Enderby looked at him. "What did make her tick, as you put it?"

"Her sense of duty. After I'd left she must have remembered something. Or been reminded. . . ." Finch's gloomily murmuring voice died as he pursued that last train of thought. "And that remark *'One doesn't gossip on such a subject.'* What on earth does that mean?"

"It's about the diamond," Enderby was quoting now. *"I saw it arrive.* That's not very enlightening either." Adding cautiously, "But it does seem to allude to the Lake of Fire."

"Does it? Can you conceive of any possible way Miss Millamont could have seen the diamond arrive?"

"No," said Enderby with spirit, "but that doesn't say that there wasn't such a way. Miss Millamont would hardly have plucked up the courage to telephone if she hadn't meant what she said. And it did take courage. . . ."

"Miss Millamont," said Finch shortly, "deserved a halo—but not yet."

"But we don't know that she's got one. I mean she may not be dead," protested Enderby, scandalised. He felt that the Scotland Yard man was taking far too much for granted. "After all," he urged, "it's not likely that Miss Millamont would have left her door unbolted. Nor that the murderer would have burst it open under the nose of my man—useless as he seems to have been."

"There's another way into her room."

"I didn't know that."

"Nor I." The car was turning into the Square.

"Then how . . .?"

"Because," said Finch, preparing to spring from the moving car, "that's the way the murderer must have come." He paused on the running board to add savagely, "One can't murder without the victim emitting *some* sound, however small and quickly ended. Much safer to wait until your man had passed and Miss Millamont was back in bed, probably with her frightened, weary old head tucked under the bedclothes."

Before Enderby could speak he was gone, Slater at his heels. Past a mildly surprised Baker, who had opened the door on hearing the car draw up. Past Kardos' closed door.

Pierce patrolling on the top floor came hurrying. More perceptive than Baker his colour receded slowly. "There's not been a sound, sir," he protested miserably. "Miss Millamont did go along to Madame Kosetti's room but I saw her safely back.'' Adding to Finch's retreating back, "I've been about the whole time. . . ."

"Like a donkey on a treadmill," Finch thought impatiently. "Only not as useful." He tried Miss Millamont's door. He called her name. Then he exchanged glances with his sergeant. Without a word spoken they proceeded to break in the lower panels. Finch put his arm in through the splintered wood and drew the bolt.

The room looked undisturbed. Its occupant's small figure was outlined beneath the bedclothes, even to her head. Only over on the far side there was a faint haze as if, behind the curtains, the window had been opened and the fog had filtered in.

Finch paused for a moment, catching his breath in a quick sigh. He crossed the floor. As he neared the bed his foot struck something. He glanced down and saw the lead figure of a faun, which he had seen earlier that evening in one of the empty attic rooms. He could guess to what use it had been put. So it did have its significance after all, he reflected grimly.

He lifted the bedclothes and looked at the mess of clotted blood and hair beneath. His gaze sharpened. Miss Millamont had been a faded blonde. Her hair had never been like this. Not this reddish yellow. Not short, silky.

He bent closer. He turned. "Get an ambulance and a doctor quick as you can, Archie. Miss Millamont's still alive."

"I'll see to it," said Enderby, who had followed the others upstairs. "I know 'em." His tone implied that he would stand no nonsense. He hurried away.

Slater joined Finch at the bedside. "What's that?" he asked. "On her head?"

"She must have put it on for warmth," said Finch. "Her new fur hat. Wired and padded, a veritable bastion of a hat. It may have saved her life. That and the fact that she was attacked through the bedclothes."

Finch crossed over and looked from the window. He saw that there was a high coping round the roof broken only where there was a window. It would have been perfectly easy for anyone to have walked in safety right round the house. Later investigation was to show that the would-be murderer had come no further than the empty room adjoining.

Outside doors were opening. There were anxious exclamations and cries and then Protheroe's voice saying what he had been told to say. "Miss Millamont has been attacked in her room. We're waiting for an ambulance." To further questions he had two answers. "I don't know, ma'am." "You'll have to ask the Inspector, sir."

And then almost abruptly the voices ceased and silence fell. Silence and an acute uneasiness. Caused by the realisation that one of those present was a killer. Had murdered ruthlessly—and, if the need arose, would do so again.

The passage whispered and grew cold on this one unspoken fact. Only Daisy's voice muttered away as if her words were an incantation against evil. ". . . fortitude you have. You have borne up in my cause and never flagged but this I have against you. You have lost your early love. Repent and do as you once did. . . ."

The police surgeon arrived, a brisk competent man with a dry manner. He did what he could for Miss Millamont. It was not much. He was anxious to get her to hospital.

"The laceration and haemorrhage are considerable," he told Finch. "Whoever wielded that lead figure meant business."

"Any idea when she'll recover consciousness?"

The doctor shrugged. "Next week—next month—never." He nodded and went briskly away.

Soon after two ambulance men arrived with a stretcher, climbing the stairs swiftly, urged on by the Superintendent.

"Think we should clear the passage?" Enderby asked. The furrows on his big face had deepened and his eyes were anxious.

Finch shook his head. "I want them to get the full effect of what's happened." He was thinking of Mrs. McGee. "Protheroe can clear a path. After that we'll just have to watch out."

Enderby nodded. "I'll do that." And the lines on his face seemed deeper than ever.

The stretcher bearers were ready. Finch opened the door. For a moment the two groups faced each other in a silence so complete that the ticking of Enderby's watch seemed an enormity.

They were all there. Finch noticed particularly Madame Kosetti in her fur coat, a shawl over her head and most of her marigold coloured hair, he suspected, left behind in her bedroom. Mrs. Bradshaw too, *her* head seemed oddly square and flat. Without her hat her hair was so thin as to have the effect of shot silk.

The static picture dissolved. Protheroe moved forward, his outstretched arms mutely asking for passageway. The inert body was carried through, the uncovered head mute testimony that Miss Millamont was still alive.

Someone, Finch thought, must just be realising that fact. Someone with black rage and fear. . . .

Then shrill and sudden Madame Kosetti's voice cried, "What is zat? What 'as she done to 'er 'air?"

Mrs. McGee's crutches slipped. She swayed towards the stretcher. She would have fallen across it had the Superintendent not shouldered her back.

The stretcher went past and out of sight down the dim and shadowy passage. No one spoke. No one moved. Just stood listening to the retreating footsteps. Mentally placing the stretcher, accompanying it on its journey. Now it had reached the landing. Now the hall. The front door opened, closed. Miss Millamont had gone from the house.

Someone in the group sighed, a long laboured sigh that was half a groan. Later Protheroe declared that it had been Mr. Gadsby but Finch was not so sure.

He and Slater returned to a consideration of the attack on Miss Millamont.

It was soon obvious that the attacker's preparations had had all the beauty of simplicity. The lead faun had been taken from one empty room. A pair of hand-knitted stockings, washed and hung on a line by Mrs. Bradshaw, from another. These stockings must have been drawn over either shoes or bare feet to avoid bringing in any tell-tale stains from the roof. They had afterwards been replaced on the line, where they might have escaped detection but for Slater's vigilance.

The only known hazard had been the patrolling police constable. The unknown hazard had been the fur hat—and it was too early to say what effect that had had on the ultimate results.

A search of Miss Millamont's room unearthed, not the Lake of Fire, but a cache under the floor. Sara, faced with its contents, had to admit to recognising, not only articles reported lost by the present community, but others that Daisy, thin-lipped with disapproval, identified as having belonged to guests long since gone from the house. A large silver button bearing the crest of Honiton in enamel she identified as having belonged to her late mistress, Mrs. Harkness.

There was too what the mice had left of Madame Rakosi's foreign library and some shreds of bright shiny paper intermixed with narrow slips of thin paper with something printed on them.

Slater squatted down to examine the latter. He read aloud, "Contentment is better than wealth. A happy heart goes all the way." He looked up smiling broadly, "Mottoes from a Christmas cracker. Can you beat it?"

"Hail, glorious edifice, stupendous work. God bless the Regent and the Duke of York," said Finch delightedly.

"I think you're both horrid," Sara declared stormily. She seemed so upset by the whole business that Finch hastened to draw an edifying picture of the great benefits bestowed on the young mice whose nests, he declared, not only had a contemporary décor but even an international culture.

It was nearly half past four when Septimus Finch and his sergeant stepped from No. 9 into a world of shifting fog. The lamps were out. All windows had long been darkened. No traffic moved and the Square was wholly empty. Even the police car had been sent away on Finch's instructions.

"Sure you know your way, Archie?" Finch asked him. His tall lounging figure looked more than life size in the surrounding murk.

"Yes, sir. It's to the left. Then at the top of the Square there's a narrow road. Go along that, and the Jolly Fisherman is on the same side. We can't miss it."

Finch chuckled sceptically. "Great last words. Enderby's I suppose." He added, "I have a feeling that Miss Millamont will survive. I didn't pass on my opinion to Miss Harkness. I don't want to alarm our murderer into trying again."

"It's rough on her having a lazy lay-about like that brother of hers," said Slater with considerable energy.

"Don't call him that if you want to get anywhere with Miss Harkness," said Finch in his soft voice.

Slater looked at his superior with genuine surprise. "But I don't want to get anywhere with Miss Harkness. I'm just sorry for her."

"Then in case you should want to get anywhere with her in the future don't call him that." Finch was peering about him curiously. From what he could make out it was not a view which would be improved by better visibility. "Tomorrow first thing I'll have the house searched for the diamond," he went on. "We may turn up something of interest. If it's only the reason why Madame Kosetti keeps her wardrobe locked."

"Queer no one has identified Tamara Lubova," said Slater. "Red hair and a retroussé nose. You'd think someone would recognise the description."

"Enderby and Mr. Bell didn't," answered Finch sadly. "I asked 'em."

Chapter 11

Returned to her bed Sara could not sleep. She was tormented by the thought of the killer in the house and by the impossibility of really believing it. The inmates of No. 9, from Madame Kosetti to Daisy, passed before her mental vision only to be repudiated one by one. And yet, she was forced to admit, the only one of whose innocence she was certain was Miss Millamont—and that only because she lay unconscious, if not dead, in hospital.

It was like a childhood game. "It isn't you! It isn't you!" But she never arrived at "It is you!"

About six o'clock she fell into an uneasy sleep. When she awoke it seemed quite natural that fog still slid stealthily across the windows. It was past eight o'clock. She sprang out of bed, dressed hurriedly and went downstairs.

The policemen standing about stiffly in the passages greeted her awkwardly. Perhaps, she reflected, they suspect me of murdering Mr. Carron and attacking poor Miss Millamont. Daisy was singing loud hymns in her bedroom and that Sara could not bear. That no one was downstairs. That everything was still to do. . . .

She raced along the flagged passage and burst into the kitchen.

Alan was there, looking relaxed and cheerful. "Thank goodness you've come," he greeted her. "I've put the plates to warm and made the toast. I was beginning to be afraid that I'd have to do the cooking as well. Daisy's right round the bend this morning."

"I know. I heard her." Sara was running her eyes over the things on the kitchen table. "Thanks awfully for doing all this." Adding, as she seized a frying pan, "I suppose you didn't have time to enquire how Miss Millamont was getting on?"

"Never gave it a thought. I expect she's dead by now."

Adding as if genuinely interested, "Would they hang anyone as old as our lot?"

Sara cried out in protest. How could any of them—even a murderer—be expected to face such a fate? She could see a woeful composite picture. Tears running down old cheeks, shaking hands and tottering steps. "Perhaps Broadmoor," she suggested in a muffled voice—and found herself shuddering away from that prospect too.

Alan, relenting, asked her what room she proposed to use as a sitting room. "Not really fancying the other one, dear."

"I thought we'd open up old Mr. Harkness' study," said Sara, thankfully seizing on this change of topic. "It'll be a bit musty I expect but that'll soon wear off."

It was a room that had been very little used since the death of the old lawyer. His widow, Daisy had explained, had not had the heart to sit there alone and Sara had kept it locked, except when really pressed for space, out of deference to what she imagined would have been her benefactor's wishes.

"D'you mind taking up the milk and seeing that the cereals are on the sideboard?" Sara asked her brother. "There's the toast too. And I'm not giving anyone breakfast in bed. If Madame Kosetti wants a meal she must come down to the dining room."

She went on cooking eggs and bacon.

Alan came back. "Everything's all right," he announced. "And everyone, except Magda Brooks, is down. Mrs. McGee came trundling in between Madame Kosetti and Mrs. Bradshaw. She looked as hangdog as a prisoner between two jailers but what it's all about I don't know. And Kardos is eating an enormous plate of cornflakes, looking madly prosperous and out of place. He may have another helping—otherwise, at the rate he's going, it won't be long before he's ready for the next course."

With things as they are all this seems an utter waste of time," Sara remarked, throwing another egg into the pan in an offhand way. "There! It's broken. I suppose I should have expected it."

"Or, better still, not dashed it in with such violence," said Alan. He added after a pause, "Sara, when this business has been cleared up, let's leave Daisy in charge of what's left and take a fortnight off. We could go to France. We've done it before on next to nothing."

Sara looked at him, exasperated. "This time it would be on less than nothing." She turned the bacon roughly and gave a cry of pain as the hot fat splashed up. It goaded her into pointing out just why in their present financial position it was out of the question. "Not," she ended bitterly, "that it isn't nice to be treated as a human being for once."

Alan's face hardened. It went cold in a way she knew and dreaded. "I suppose it's that fellow, Slater, who has made you think you are one," he said with a vicious glance. "I must say I scarcely expected to have a policeman as a brother-in-law. But he looks healthy enough. I believe they have to reach a certain standard physically. Mentally, too, although this I find hard to believe."

He left the kitchen suddenly. Shutting the door with a violence that matched Sara's own feelings. She stared after him, torn between fury and unhappiness.

She turned back to the stove and, dishing Kardos' eggs and bacon roughly onto a plate, carried it along to the dining room.

A few minutes later Daisy appeared in the kitchen. "That Inspector has just arrived," she announced, looking at Sara in what the girl thought was a slightly dotty way. "He says I can't do the bedrooms because he'll be up there, so I may as well get on here."

She plunged across the kitchen to the sink, muttering, "At least it'll keep me away from that Mr. Kardos. Waylaid me he did. Wanted to ask me something about Mr. Gadsby. I didn't wait to hear what. The cheek of it. And what's he been up to—looking for all the world like a cream-fed cat?"

"He does look a bit complacent," said Sara uneasily, "but I can't think why."

Daisy turned, up to her elbows in soapy water, "D'you reckon we ought to warn him—Mr. Gadsby, I mean. Acting queer he may be, popping up all over the place like a Jack-in-the-box but he means no harm by it. Which is more than I can say for some people—for all they're so free with their money."

After a couple of hours' sleep Finch was up again. He telephoned to the local hospital and enquired after Miss Millamont's health. The house surgeon, who spoke to him, said that at least she was alive and that was something. The haemorrhage, it appeared, had not been as serious as had been feared.

He reassured Finch as to the patient's safety. "Superintendent Enderby insists on being in the same room with her." He added plaintively, "I've put a muslin screen round him but I still wish he wouldn't."

This would have been enough to put Finch in a good temper had it been necessary. As it was he decided to save it up for Slater. It continued to amuse him whilst he wrote his report for Scotland Yard and made out a list of people about whom he wanted enquiries made—and these included an urgent enquiry into the death of Harry Brooks.

Archie Slater slept badly. As this was an almost unprecedented event he felt correspondingly aggrieved. He drank several rather nasty cups of coffee, refused his food and received Finch's story about the Superintendent with a chilly smile.

Only when he saw his superior's commiserating expression did he realise that his behaviour had given fuel to his chief's absurd delusion that he was personally interested in Sara Harkness.

By nine o'clock they were on their way to No. 9. Daisy, looking sour and thin lipped, let them into the house. "I happened to be near," she said in a grumbling voice. "I was just going upstairs to do the bedrooms."

"You won't be able to do them just now," said Finch. "We shall be up there most of the morning. But if you can spare a moment there's something I want to ask you."

"Ask away," said Daisy in a reckless way as if he had suggested her participation in some orgy. "If I'm not to do the work I'm paid for I suppose I've time to waste."

"I was discussing Mrs. Winfield's death with Miss Harkness. She remembered your saying that you thought the deceased had had something on her mind?"

Daisy stared. "That I never." She corrected herself. "Now I come to think of it, you're right. Mrs. Winfield was a proper nosey-parker. Then, all of a sudden, she seemed to lose interest in things. Just sat around, absent-minded like."

Finch was keenly interested. "For how long before her death was she like this?"

"I can't recall."

"D'you remember if it was after Madame Rakosi's death or before?"

"It was after." Daisy was growing restive. "But don't you go getting any idea that she was upset by Madame Rakosi's death. We could all have died and she wouldn't have turned a hair."

She disappeared in the direction of the kitchen.

Sergeant Protheroe, who had been waiting to report to Finch, stepped forward. He gave it as his opinion that the maidservant was not all there. "She never went to bed, for every time I passed I could hear her banging about in her room. About seven o'clock she began to sing hymns in a loud voice. When she came out just now she said something about evil not prevailing and that Miss Harkness must be kept out of it. Seemed to be worrying about her safety.''

While Finch was giving Protheroe some instructions, Sara came hurrying into the hall. She greeted Finch, then asked anxiously after Miss Millamont.

''I overslept and I haven't had a moment to telephone.'' She felt awkward with Slater after what her brother had said. She did not speak to him at once and, after a little, it seemed too late.

''We must just go on hoping,'' said Finch sententiously. ''Meanwhile I hope that you'll be careful and not do anything rash. For instance I'd rather that you didn't go out alone in this fog.''

''Daisy told me that she couldn't do the rooms?'' Sara glanced surreptitiously at Slater but he was not looking in her direction.

''I'm sorry about that but I'm going to search the house,'' said Finch solemnly. Inwardly he was diverted by their behaviour. ''So, if any of the rooms, drawers or cupboards, are locked perhaps I could have the keys.''

''Of course. I'm going to use one of the rooms on this floor as an office. I have the key here. The others are in my desk. I'll get them for you.''

But this Finch would not allow, realising that it would be an ordeal for the girl to enter the room where Mr. Carron had died.

Left alone Sara unlocked the door of the study. A mingled smell of damp and mould came out to meet her. She stood slightly aghast. Convicted once again of inadequacy. Anyone else, she reflected ruefully, would have remembered to keep the room aired.

She crossed the floor and opened the shutters, shivering a little, her nose wrinkled in distaste. She looked about her—at the leather chairs, the red Turkey carpet on the floor, the pale water colours painted by Mr. Gadsby of seabirds treading delicately on the wet sands at dawn. At the books imprisoned behind glass doors. Doubly imprisoned, she reflected, because of their subject matter.

It occurred to her suddenly that perhaps she should have given them to some library for the benefit of students of law. Or, since she could not afford the gesture, sell them perhaps. They were probably as useful today as they had been when they were published.

She walked over to one of the bookcases. There were she knew a little group of books that had belonged to Mrs. Harkness, Proust, D. H. Lawrence, Chesterton. A fat exercise book full of cookery recipes, some cut from magazines, some in bold slanting handwriting.

She pulled this book out and turned the pages. They were, she thought, very ordinary dishes. On one page she found written, "Geoffrey, unlike James, does not like the English boiled potato."

Sara's first feeling was of amusement. James, she imagined, must have been Millicent Harkness' first husband. Then it struck her that there was something odd about the sentence. She did not bother to track it down but turned to the other books.

Her eyes ran idly over the titles.

"Laws of England in 31 volumes by the Earl of Halsbury." "Lord Simonds on Halsbury's Laws of England"—now grown to thirty-six volumes. Anson's "Law of Contract." A whole row of "Public General Acts and Measures."

She saw a fat, rather squat book. "Everyman's Own Lawyer."—A handy Book of the Principles of Law and Equity by a Barrister.

It seemed rather an odd sort of book to find in the shelves of a fully trained lawyer. She pulled it out. Her eyes widened. The book had been published first in 1863. This was the 68th edition, published in 1955.

And Mr. Harkness had died in 1949.

She looked on the fly leaf. It was blank and gave no clue to the owner's identity. She thought that the most likely person to have bought it would have been the widow. Looking at the number of editions, Sara saw that since the First World War it had been reprinted, at a rough estimate, every three years so that, had this copy been bought in 1955, '56 or even '57, it would still have been this edition.

Sara ruffled through the leaves. Then she began to turn them one by one, at first carefully, then more hurriedly but still with a dogged patience born of an illogical feeling that something would come of the search.

Somewhere about the middle of the book she came on part of a letter. It appeared to have been written in a great hurry—or perhaps under the stress of some strong emotion. A suggestion borne out by the fact that the sheet of paper appeared to have been torn roughly in two down its length and then again across, making four unequal pieces of which only this one had survived.

A search later through the rest of the book disclosed no more.

For a long moment Sara stared down at the writing. Writing that at first was as incomprehensible and frightening as would have been the immense bones of some unidentifiable creature stumbled upon on a commonplace but lonely ramble.

Yet there was a familiarity about the letter. She recognised that it lay in the handwriting. She had seen its counterpart only a few minutes before in the book of cookery recipes. The letter then had been written by old Mrs. Harkness.

She realised then what had been odd in that sentence about the potatoes. Mrs. Harkness had written *English* potato as if she herself had been a foreigner.

Sara stared blankly and cold fingers trailed along her spine as her thoughts came to their logical conclusion.

There had been something bizarre in the idea of Tamara Lubova's connection with No. 9. Which one had she been? Where had she come from? How did she get here?

Now, in part, the questions had been answered. Tamara Lubova and the doctor's widow from Torquay had been one and the same. The doctor's widow and Millicent (why Millicent?) Harkness had been one. That was what Mr. Carron would have told her had he lived. That had been the romance to which he had alluded. And the diamond . . . ? The Lake of Fire had belonged to her. And now . . .

I leave my entire estate to Sara Dorette Harkness.

But I don't want it, she cried in silent revolt. Of all the people in this house I'm probably the only one who does not want it.

Sara might have broken into hysterical laughter, had she not been assailed with an acute prescience of disaster. It was as if she had already a hideous notion of what she was about to learn.

She turned again to the letter.

The words that had been on first sight like something from an incomplete puzzle, unconsecutive and baffling, now on second inspection made a dreadful sort of truth.

The letter breathed a bitter hurt and disillusionment. It bore no form of address and appeared to be the second page . . . and an unsatisfactory one at that, since it had been torn up and discarded.

What there was of it read——

> *spied on me. Been caught*
> *act of stealing from me*
> > *Yes, that I can promise*
> *your secret. In return you*
> *keep mine.*
> > *I realise that this has been*
> *home for a considerable time but*
> *cannot allow you to return. Is*
> *enough that I shall be reminded*
> *you every time I look around*
> *walls? So stay*
> *in Hollo*

I shall be reminded of you every time I look around these walls. The words repeated themselves in Sara's mind. Almost against her will, and like a person in the grip of a nightmare, she turned her head to look at the painting over the mantelpiece.

Was it Mr. Gadsby who had attempted to steal the diamond? Had he been ordered to leave the house and then, in deference to their long friendship, had Mrs. Harkness allowed him to give the bad temper of his dog as the reason for his departure?

Sara stiffened.

Mr. Gadsby had attended the funeral of the woman whose friendship he had betrayed. Had he stolen the diamond then? Or had he obtained possession of it later, after she, Sara, had allowed him to return?

Perfidious Mr. Gadsby.

Cunning Mr. Gadsby.

But was his guilt certain?

Sara looked again at the letter.

"So stay . . . in Hollo. . . ." It was not so easy here to fill in the missing words. For all that they constituted the last, the final link in the indictment.

Mr. Gadsby's letter, asking if he might return, had been written from a place called Hollodale. Sara might not have remembered it except that he had mentioned it several times since. Explained why he preferred the old spelling of the name. Told her that it had been a beautiful place. He had enjoyed eating the local salmon. His old dog had been buried where the heather and the gorse . . .

Sara closed her eyes a moment. Nothing remained now but

to give this piece of paper to the Inspector. Tell him what she knew——

She turned quite briskly to replace the book. Then she paused, hesitating.

But could she. . . ? Unless she was absolutely certain, could she. . . ?

Suppose the letter, the whole letter, had had some quite other interpretation? Suppose there might be some innocent explanation? An explanation known to someone in the house and perhaps only revealed when it was too late? When Mr. Gadsby . . . ?

She shuddered away from the thought of either hanging or Broadmoor.

But if the letter did have an innocent explanation, who would know? Who else could she ask? Whom could she trust with the story of her find?

She could have trusted the tall, lantern-jawed young sergeant, Archie Slater, if he had not been a police officer. If, behind him, had not been the Inspector. And Sara found Finch a very alarming person for all that he was outwardly so amiable and sleepy looking.

There seemed, she decided wearily, only Daisy. Daisy at her most unpredictable. Even so, surely she would be able to recall Mr. Gadsby's departure from No. 9, and whether there had been anything strange about it.

Her mind made up, Sara replaced "Everyman's Own Lawyer" and closed the door of the bookcase. Her heart gave a sudden lurch. She could have sworn that, for a split second, someone had been reflected in the glass.

She ran over to the door and looked out. The hall was quiet and empty. "I'm getting jumpy," she thought. She stood for a moment looking about but the whole place was still. It was only her own imagination that suggested that the stillness had a watchful quality that had not been there before.

She stiffened as she heard someone coming, soft-footed, towards the hall.

It was Mr. Kardos. He wore his overcoat. He carried his hat in one hand and a small tea tray in the other. "I bring it from my bedroom," he said handsomely, "but there was no one in the kitchen to receive it." His eyes explored the room behind her. "Now I go out. With so much disturbance it is necessary you understand. I find myself a comfortable hotel." His tone was a reproach. "Perhaps even," he added largely, "I do not return for the luncheon."

He divided a sad valedictory smile between her and the room. Gave her the tray. Put on his hat, opened the front door and walked out into the fog.

Sara found herself staring once more at a closed door. She shivered involuntarily.

Chapter 12

The Chief Constable was annoyed at what he considered the thoughtlessness of Superintendent Enderby in leaving him to deal single handed with the reporters and camera men who had come swarming (his own exaggerated description of the event) into Seamarsh.

Because he was annoyed he had fixed half past ten as the earliest moment at which he could spare the men to carry out the search of No. 9. This annoyed Finch. He was filling in the time prowling about the bedrooms on the second and top floors of the house. Slater and Protheroe were with him.

Daisy's bedroom was a place so bare, bleak and empty that it was a wonder anyone could occupy it.

Mr. Gadsby's room was almost as characteristic of its owner as was Daisy's but in a completely different manner. It was a pale room but rather attractive and undeniably comfortable. The walls were distempered a pale green. A grey carpet lay on the floor. There were some shelves full of calf-bound books and pale water colours hung on the walls.

"That's Sidmouth," said Slater. "My uncle's vicar down there. And that looks like the fishing boats at Brixham."

"And these others, I imagine, were painted in the Highlands of Scotland. You remember Enderby said he went there to live for a time with his dog."

Protheroe had been opening and closing the drawers of a tallboy. He gave a sudden exclamation. He had found three silver buttons bearing the crest of Honiton.

"So Daisy was mistaken," Finch commented. "That button we found hidden in Miss Millamont's room belonged to Mr. Gadsby, and not to the late Mrs. Harkness."

"She's been dead for five years, sir," said Protheroe weightedly.

"It was a natural enough mistake." He dropped the buttons back into the drawer.

Finch, who was a tolerant man, reflected that if he had to see much of Protheroe, he would have to slap him down—hard. He sent a constable to get the key of Madame Kosetti's wardrobe.

They went upstairs to the attics and wandered through the unoccupied rooms. By daylight they looked as if someone with squirrel-like propensities and a slightly crazy view of what was necessary had intended to move in. Had then abandoned the project, leaving behind such seemingly unrelated articles as a broken-down day bed, Fox's "Book of Martyrs" and a painter's easel.

Protheroe was inclined to be shocked. Finch was amused and Slater inattentive. He kept wondering moodily what he had done to offend Sara.

"You know," said Finch suddenly, "this really is the answer. What's wanted to make happy old people's homes are incompetent, kindhearted and slightly highbrow young women to run them."

The constable came back flushed with battle and the key of Madame Kosetti's wardrobe. It was a huge affair with a centre, half shelves, half drawers. The shelves were filled with letters, photographs and documents. Slater, who had a working knowledge of German, began to go through them.

Protheroe, who had drawn the curtains back as far as they would go, remarked, "The old ladies were thick as thieves this morning—all three of them. Went into breakfast together. Came out and went into the lounge together."

"That," Finch remarked, peering at the cluttered objects on the dressing table, "wasn't so much a sign of friendship as of caution."

Presently Slater gave a sudden angry exclamation. He had discovered Madame Kosetti's secret. She was a comparatively wealthy woman, receiving money regularly from the continent.

"The mean old so and so," he exploded. "Still paying her three pounds ten a week and, from all accounts, bewailing every penny of it. But how did she manage to have this money without anyone knowing?"

"I don't suppose she had it until the last few years when the Commission, appointed to unscramble the assets taken over by Hitler, got round to returning them to their original owners."

Miss Millamont's bedroom had been sealed by Finch before he had left the house. The seal was unbroken. For all that he stood quite still in the entrance for a long minute, observing the location of every item.

"Interesting if someone had thought it worth while to come in by the window again," he murmured.

Protheroe was shaken by this evidence of incompetence in high places. "I know the old ladies had to come up to this floor for their clothes but I could have had a man out on the roof," he told Finch reproachfully.

Finch turned his head and looked at him. "But then we shouldn't have known that there was anything to take, should we, Sergeant?" he said in his soft drawling voice.

He walked forward into the room.

The dressing table was undisturbed. The short lengths of black cotton, which Finch had taken from Miss Millamont's work basket and shut into the cracks of the drawers, were still there.

He went over to the chest of drawers. Here, clearly shown in the fine layer of dust which lay on its surface, was the mark where something had stood.

"Just what might have been expected," said Finch. "Someone thought it worth while to crawl along behind the coping and remove a photograph."

He glanced at his wrist watch. Another twenty minutes to go before the other Seamarsh police would arrive. Like the Chief Constable, only for a different reason, he thought that Superintendent Enderby could have been better employed than sitting behind a muslin screen at the hospital.

A constable arrived with a note from the police station. It contained a message from Scotland Yard.

Finch read it. He looked amused. "I shall have to leave you two for a few minutes. While I'm gone you can search for the photograph taken from Miss Millamont's room—or a copy of it."

He ran down the stairs. On the first floor he walked along to Mrs. Brooks' room and knocked.

He went in. "Why did you tell me that you were a widow?"

Mrs. Brooks turned first white, then red. "How dare you pry into my affairs," she gasped, gripping the back of a chair as if for support.

"How dare you tell me a pack of bare-faced lies?"

"I—I——" Magda's voice stammered to a halt. She opened a cigarette box and took one out. Finch lighted it for her. When she spoke again she had recovered from the shock his words had given her. "Harry ran away with a chambermaid from the hotel in which we were staying. A skinny yellow haired girl as common as dirt."

"And you wouldn't divorce him? Was that it?"

She looked at him squarely, blowing smoke from her elegant nose. "And I wouldn't divorce him. That *was* it."

"And that was the reason for your quarrels with your uncle?"

She winced and her expression changed. She said, looking down at the cigarette in her hand, "Yes—yet when he died Harry and his divorce seemed of no importance."

Finch looked at her quizzically, "Well then?"

"How can I do it now that I've said Harry was dead?"

"But he can't be dead in South Africa?" You could go back there."

She shrugged. "Perhaps I will. Perhaps I won't."

Finch left her feeling that she was far nearer to doing what her uncle had wanted than she would admit—even to herself.

He went upstairs. Slater had found an unmounted photograph hidden behind one of a young cavalry officer. Sergeant Protheroe uncovered a companion picture padding the lining of Mrs. Bradshaw's summer hat.

The two photographs were identical. A little faded, yellowing round the edges and dated 1934. They showed the head and bare shoulders of a beautiful but mature woman. Large laughing eyes, a charming smile and the most appealing of noses, clear cut, and undeniably tip-tilted.

So this was Tamara Lubova, Finch thought. He put her age down as forty-four or five. He wondered again what had happened to mar her beauty. He asked Protheroe if it reminded him of anyone.

The sergeant shook his head. "One couldn't forget that face, sir."

Finch slipped the two copies into his pocket. "We'll go down and tackle those three old witches," he said.

The old ladies were still in the lounge. They were not talking. Madame Kosetti sat close to the fire. She looked years older. Her face had crumbled into a tragic and intricate ruin. Her lips moved continuously and her eyes were dull, and lost in the puffy fat which surrounded them.

A newspaper lay on her lap. The late Mr. Carron stared up from its front page but it was disregarded by the old ladies. They had other, more immediate anxieties.

Mrs. Bradshaw was knitting. Of the three she seemed least affected by recent events. Her fingers moved incessantly on the circular needle as she knitted one of her strangely shaped garments and her eyes, darting anxiously about, were as bright and shining as prunes.

Mrs. McGee looked ill. Her hard mannish face was plainer than ever. Her eyes were swollen and her cheeks roughened with tears. Occasionally she glanced at her two companions but she did not speak. She had given up expecting any comfort from them and in this she was not disappointed.

Finch, with Slater and Protheroe behind him, might have been thought to have made a formidable trio. The old ladies gave no sign that they were even aware of their entry into the lounge. Only Madame Kosetti by sheer will power seemed to reassemble her former self. Her face smoothed itself out. Her lips were still and her eyes acquired something of their old fire and lustre.

Finch made no attempt to lead up to his subject. He thrust a photograph at each of its owners. "Who is this?"

Madame Kosetti looked at it unmoved. "It is me—in my young days."

"So I have always understood," agreed Mrs. Bradshaw. For the moment she seemed to have foregone the spiritual reassurance of her late husband.

"And you, Mrs. McGee? Who do you say this is?"

The woman in the chair shook her head. "The photograph's not mine," she said in a peevish voice. She made a feeble attempt to push it away.

"That was not what I asked you." Finch continued to hold it inexorably before her.

Mrs. McGee turned her head helplessly from side to side. Her eyes wandered feverishly. Inadvertently they met Finch's and the battle was lost.

"It's Millicent Harkness," she whispered brokenly. "Millie. . . ."

Mrs. Bradshaw tottered to her feet. "You wicked woman. You have killed Sara."

"On the contrary, if you had the good sense to tell me earlier you might have saved Miss Millamont's life," said Finch, reflecting that here, in his love for his foreign born wife, lay the explanation as to why the staid elderly solicitor had become another Scarlet Pimpernel.

"Then Miss Millamont *is* dead?" Mrs. McGee turned on

the others. "I kept telling you—I said that there was no need for Sara to know about the diamond but you wouldn't listen."

"It's other people knowing that worries me," said Mrs. Bradshaw, glaring at Mrs. McGee and inelegantly scratching under her hat with the end of the knitting needle. "There's the murderer—and I wouldn't trust that brother of hers."

"At least," said Mrs. McGee, with a dolorous sniff, "I had the decency to keep my promise and destroy my copy of Millie."

"Only," retorted Mrs. Bradshaw, "because you didn't care for her as Freda and I did."

"Oh, be quiet both of you," said Madame Kosetti crossly. "It is done now." She folded her hands on her stomach and looked at Finch. "What did you want to know?"

"I want to know about the diamond." Finch turned to Mrs. McGee. "I imagine that Mrs. Harkness told you about it when she lay dying."

"Yes. Until then I had no idea of her past history."

"I knew," said Madame Kosetti with a kind of sour triumph. "We had known the same people—only from a somewhat different viewpoint."

"You had the diamond and someone stole it from you?"

"I never actually had it. I never ever saw it. I—I didn't dare," Mrs. McGee's voice was muffled. Two tears rolled down her hard red cheeks. "I'm ashamed to admit it but when I heard of it I was bitterly envious. I kept thinking of the fortune I could make if only I could have borrowed the diamond for a little while. How I would pawn it and then redeem it. No one would have been the wiser." She looked with blurred eyes at Finch. "I daresay you can't understand the temptation but it was days before I conquered it. The funeral was over. Mr. Carron had written the letter to Sara." She paused, when she spoke again her voice was a hoarse whisper. "Millicent kept her jewellery in a green morocco case. It had a very large square knob on top. The Lake of Fire was in there. It had a trick opening. Millie explained as best she could. I had a great difficulty in manipulating it. . . ." The hoarse voice grated to a standstill.

"And when you did open it, the diamond was gone?"

Mrs. McGee whispered the one word, "Yes."

Finch nodded. Then he asked what seemed a totally irrelevant question. "Did Mr. Gadsby attend Mrs. Harkness' funeral?"

Madame Kosetti answered. "Yes, he did. I remember I was surprised at his coming all that way. So expensive and not really necessary.'' Her voice was tart but her eyes searched Finch's face anxiously as if to fathom the reason for the question.

Finch himself was silent a moment. Then he said softly, almost as if he spoke to himself. ''So that was it. That was what Miss Millamont saw arrive. Not the diamond but a train bringing an unexpected visitor.''

As the three men left the room Mrs. McGee's tearful voice followed them. ''It was not so bad as long as my husband was alive. I could persuade myself that I had only to tell him and he would put everything right. But after he died and Sara was in such financial difficulties . . .''

Finch had halted in his tracks. ''Did you ever tell your husband?''

Mrs. McGee shook her head. ''I never dared. He would have been so angry, so disgusted. . . .''

Sara had left No. 9 by the back door. She carried a large shopping bag. *If the police ask where you're going you can tell them you have to do the shopping.* Alan had said that. He'd refused to leave the house with her but had said that he would catch her up.

She had not liked the arrangement but she had felt too worn out, too buffeted by argument to stand any more.

And there had been some force in Alan's argument that, if they were seen leaving together, Inspector Finch might grow suspicious, insist even on sending someone with them. And how then would they be able to tackle Daisy on the question of Mr. Gadsby's guilt or innocence?

So here she was, hurrying through the fog, her bruised mind going over and over the recent interview with Alan with the weary monotony of a squirrel in a revolving cage.

She had found him comfortably reading a newspaper by one of the radiators in the dining room. He had been as wildly excited by her find as she had expected. His eyes had been like blue sparkling ice, as he paced up and down. Words had flowed from him but always in a frantic whispering as if, even in the midst of his pre-occupation, he had recognised the need for secrecy.

Diamonds had reached an all time high in the auction rooms. With the money they could live on Spain's Costa Brava. That was the place nowadays. Buy a villa. Have their friends out to stay. Names tripped off his tongue. A dissolute middle-aged actor. A man who was known to have made a fortune from strip-tease clubs and was reputed to have made another from vice houses. A young woman who had married a senile old man for his money and entertained her lovers in front of his imperceptive rheumy old eyes. The two young men with whom he had been mixed up in the rent racket and with whom he had sworn that he had broken.

Sara had listened in horror. She had not lost touch with the smart world so long that she did not recognise those names.

Alan had seemed suddenly to become aware of the magnitude of his indiscretion. He had stopped his wild pacings to demand, still in that frantic whispering, exactly what she intended to do with the diamond.

When he had heard that the one thing on which she had decided was that she was not going to give him money so that he could give up working, he had flown into a suppressed passion of such violence that it had frightened her.

He had seemed to combine with his present grievance everything he had ever held against her—and this had included her behaviour last night and what he described as her laughable last-ditch attempts to attract Archie Slater.

Then he had changed from anger to a pleading so desperate that his face had grown pale and his eyes had held something of horror and a sick despair. Then as suddenly he had stopped that too, staring at her in a strange, rather terrifying manner.

It was after this that Sara had been seized with a sudden sense of danger. It had been accompanied by a strong conviction that someone else was near them, listening, plotting perhaps.

Although there had been no one in the hall when Alan had thrown open the door the feeling of danger had persisted. It had even infected Alan. His voice had dropped still further. His gaze had become uneasy, almost furtive.

It was then that he had urged on her the necessity for caution. If they were to get to Daisy they must leave the house separately. Not be seen together. He would give her five minutes' start and then catch up with her.

At the bottom of the Square Sara took a trolley bus. She sat stiffly, filled with an absurd conviction that it was filled with sinister people, all conscious of the fact that she was the legal owner of the Lake of Fire. All silent and all watching her. Waiting to see where she left the bus so that they could follow her.

She got out at the fish market and the trolley rattled on its way. She had a last picture of two rows of silent people. A fat man, who had been standing, took her seat. That was the only change. The trolley was hidden almost at once by fog.

She walked up and down waiting for Alan. It was a district of small shops. She could hear voices about her and people passed, indefinite in the fog. It was cold with the mist swirling around her—and it was lonely. Once the trolley bus had gone she was aware of her loneliness.

Another trolley rattled along, then another—and still Alan had not come. It struck her suddenly that five minutes was a long time and a single person not the easiest of quarries to find.

She decided that she could not wait any longer.

She crossed the empty fish market and passed into a maze of small streets. Pedestrians grew fewer. Cars crawled past only occasionally.

In the silent obscurity of the fog Sara's thoughts drifted away to her own concerns. How could she arrange matters so that Alan could benefit from the sale of the diamond? (Always supposing it was found and turned out to be even half as valuable as he had visualised!) How could he have his share and yet not be able to squander it? And those friends . . . ?

She walked on, rejecting each plan almost as soon as she had thought of it. She felt wretched, depressed and anxious.

She came to the dead part of the town. Busy enough in the summer the shops and amusement arcades were closed now for the winter. Invisible in the fog she recreated them in her mind's eye. The Lightship Café. Jack's Oyster Bar, Ma's Eel & Pie Shop, Harrison's Waxworks . . .

She turned into a narrow road between high walls. A warehouse on one side, an amusement park on the other.

Later she could not pin point the exact moment when she had known that someone was behind her in the fog. She knew only that gradually, insidiously, on the soft silent paws of the fog she had been invaded by fear and the consciousness of small sounds.

In a place where every footfall was hollow there had been faint echoes that might well not have been hers. A clandestine whisper of cloth brushing against one of the high walls.

She turned and stood still, trying desperately to see into the fog. At once a chilling silence fell. "Alan!" she called experimentally. And heard the name run backwards from her, echoing eerily. When they had died away there was no further sound.

The fog clung to her cold face like cobwebs. Swirled about her, assuming strange shapes, none of them human. It did not shake her conviction that someone was there, quite silent, just beyond her range of vision.

In this deserted place she felt that it would be no good calling for help. Rash to the point of folly to step forward and confront her silent pursuer. There remained then only the bleak prospect of continuing her journey.

She turned and hurried on.

There were two courses open to her. She could take the long way round, where shops and houses offered a dubious and uncertain degree of safety. Or she could do as she had planned with Alan. Take the short cut through the old railway tunnel.

Comforting herself with the thought of the people—and the safety—she would find once she had reached the chapel, she decided to keep to her original plan walking so fast now that it was almost a run. Still she could not outpace the uneasy conviction that someone followed silently behind her.

Fear began to gather around her, moving in and out of the quiet buildings. Phantoms seemed to crowd in on her, inching closer and closer, then dissolving into the nothingness of mist with here a locked door and there the blank stare of a vacant window.

The railway tunnel had been constructed originally so that seaborne coal could be taken from the jetty to the railway station on the other side of the town. It had had a single track on which open trucks had run. It was short and dark, the walls pierced with an occasional recess like an upended coffin, for the safety of any railway ganger who might have been working there.

Sara plunged into its dark mouth. Then halted suddenly. This time her strategy was rewarded. She heard a single, incautious footfall, soft, furtive and hurriedly stilled. She looked back but the damp, shifting curtain of fog blocked her vision.

She went on in sudden panic. And now her pursuer was running. The footsteps, tiptoeing and infinitely terrifying, were gaining on her. Her heart pounded and her breath was short. She came to a standstill, a cry of fear breaking from her lips.

A man was standing in one of the recesses. Standing quite still, looking at her. An enormous man with a broad face, a rudimentary button of a nose and two small shrewd eyes.

He spoke. "Sorry I scared you, lady." His teeth shone out in a wide, good-natured grin.

Sara felt sick with relief. She saw that he was a fisherman wearing the traditional navy blue sweater and big sea boots. "I seem to scare easily today but it began before I saw you. Someone seems to be following me."

The man's smile vanished as abruptly as if a tap had been

turned. "You pass me, lady." He motioned with his head. "I'll sort him out for you."

For a moment curiosity held Sara gazing after him. She saw for a moment his comfortable homely bulk filling the tunnel. Then the place echoed with sound. Running footsteps, the fisherman's voice bellowing, " 'Ere! Come back you!" and his heavy pounding footfalls in pursuit.

Sara began to run in the other direction. Across the little public garden she sped, the little garden where in fine weather old people sat on the seats and mothers pushed their prams down gravelled paths. She emerged into another street.

The building which had once been the town's aquarium rose suddenly before her. She raced up the three steps leading to the entrance and pushed open the heavy mahogany door. She heaved a sigh of relief. She had reached her goal. She was inside the Chapel of the Watchful People.

She hesitated for a moment, wondering if she should lock the door. She remembered Alan somewhere behind her and decided against it. She looked about her.

The walls and ceiling of the wide passage in which she found herself were papered in gold. A thick purple carpet was under her feet. It all seemed as she remembered it, yet something was wrong.

For a moment she did not know what it was. Then she realised that the whole place was wrapped in silence. Not the breathing silence of a praying congregation but the silence of emptiness.

Perhaps even Daisy——

With a sinking heart Sara walked down the passage. She pushed aside the heavy velvet curtains at the end and found herself looking into the chapel itself.

Chapter 13

Two years ago when she had come to the Chapel of the Watchful People with Alan there had been lights everywhere. Those which had not been burning already had been switched on by Mr. Gadsby so that everything could be seen to its best advantage. Brass, gilt, embroidery, all had shone with an almost hypnotic brilliance.

Today there were no lights. It was gloomy where she stood. Further in it was not much better. The fog seemed to have got in and, although what light there was came in through the glass dome at the far end, everything down there remained curiously vague and indistinct. Filled with a sad grey light, shot here and there with the glitter of gold or brass.

There was a group of oddly dressed people standing together on the low platform at the end. She saw them with a stab of relief, tinged with surprise; for the absence of any sound had convinced her that the place was empty. Then she realised that they were not real people but the plaster figures to which Mr. Gadsby had taken exception. She was alone.

Behind the figures was the door through which Mr. Gadsby had appeared. She wondered whether Daisy was in the room beyond it. As she walked down the central aisle to investigate, remembered objects came to view.

The walls hung in varying shades of mauve and purple velvet. The shallow steps which led to the platform. The long table covered with a handsome velvet cloth. The four winged beasts, crouching one at each corner. The throne-like chair behind the table from which the chapel's founder, Mr. Jolly, must once have officiated. The seven brass candlesticks on seven golden plinths. Seven electric light bulbs shining out from seven golden stars. The great gilt cross which seemed to float high overhead, but which she knew was, in reality, fixed to the rails of the gallery running under the dome. The angels higher still, blowing their golden trumpets from every corner.

Sombre magnificence she had called it to Archie Slater. He came to mind suddenly, tall, calm and infinitely reassuring.

She wished suddenly, passionately, that he were here. Or, alternatively, that she had never embarked on this venture. As far as she could see all that she had done was to endanger Daisy's life and her own. Yet suppose that it had not, after all, been Mr. Gadsby behind her in the tunnel? Suppose the letter . . . ?

She was caught up in the same dilemma. It seemed to have been with her a long time. Like some old legend the question of Mr. Gadsby's guilt continued to haunt without convincing.

She mounted the low platform. The plaster figures, all some five feet high, were very near to her now. A theatrical looking group of Biblical characters, too highly coloured and with staring lacklustre eyeballs.

The focal point of the group was a statue of the Virgin Mary seated pensively in a niche. There was something rather charming about her, a youthful and virginal quality that touched the heart. She differed from the rest in that she wore real clothes. A rich blue velvet mantle and under it a white robe richly embroidered with gold thread and sewn with small pieces of looking glass which picked up and reflected the light and colour about her.

Mr. Gadsby, Sara thought, might have been right in dismissing the other figures as inartistic. She was conscious of a distinct liking for this one.

She noticed that the blue cloak was disarranged at one side. She would have put out a hand to straighten it if she had not been pierced suddenly with a stab of terror.

She became aware of the silence and the isolation. The place now had a claustral gloom. No sound broke in on her and every nerve seemed to be sending out messages of alarm.

The door beyond the plaster figures opened suddenly, making her heart jump and thud.

Daisy came through carrying a cloth and a bucket. She saw Sara and her expression grew sour. "If you want me to come back and get lunch I can't do it," she said, eyeing her young mistress antagonistically. "There's no one else turned up to do the cleaning. It's the weather I suppose. But you'd think they'd have more thought for their immortal souls. . . ."

Sara listened with a feeling of stupefaction. It seemed incredible that Daisy should stand there, so familiar. So exactly as usual in her dark cotton frock and working apron, cleaning materials in her hands and acid complaints on her lips.

"Daisy, stop!" Sara caught her by the arm. "This is important. Nothing to do with lunch." She spoke rapidly and her voice sounded small and lost in the empty hall. "I just want to ask you something. It's about Mr. Gadsby and a letter I found in the study." She broke off to enquire if she, Daisy, had known that Mrs. Harkness had been Tamara Lubova.

Daisy stared—"If she was she never told me." She gave a harsh cackle of laughter.

"Oh hush!" Sara implored. "And listen. We have so little time." The memory of those footsteps retreating down the tunnel came back to her. She glanced uneasily towards the curtains which masked the entrance to the hall. How far behind her was Mr. Gadsby?

Quickly she began to tell the story of her find and of her reason for coming to the chapel.

As she spoke she found her attention distracted by the plaster figures. They seemed to be listening, peering at her with every variety of expression. A ghostly host, from the gaunt wild eyed John the Baptist at her right to the red-haired Judas Iscariot on her left.

The thought crossed her mind that perhaps Mr. Gadsby had been wrong in dismissing them as tawdry. Wasn't there something abominable about Judas' foxy face so close to her own? Something reassuring about the Sons of Thunder watching her reflectively out of the clear eyes of fishermen set in brick red weather-beaten faces?

Daisy was staring with astonishment, oblivious of the fact that she still held the bucket and cloth. "Him? That poor softy? I don't believe it." Which, more politely put, was rather what Sara herself had felt.

"But thinking back, do you remember anything odd about his departure from No. 9?"

Daisy was silent a moment, absent-mindedly wiping her hands on the cloth she held. She said at last, "Only that the mistress wasn't well that morning. I remember it because Mr. Gadsby was upset and kept hanging about, hoping she'd come down. In the end he nearly lost the train and that dog of his tried to bite the taxi driver." Adding obtusely, "But the mistress made it all right two days later. She wrote him a long letter. Shut herself in the study all one afternoon to do it. I know because she sent it by registered post and I had to go to the post office with it.''

Sara's heart sank. So there it was! The Mr. Gadsby she knew had ceased to exist. In his place was only the monster, the killer who had moved unsuspected on his dark ventures through the dreary rooms of No. 9.

Said she sadly, ''And today I found a bit of the rough copy of that letter.''

''D'you mean . . . ?'' Daisy's face was mottled. Her eyes stared in consternation. ''There's some mistake. It's not possible.''

Sara shivered. Was it her imagination? or had the chapel grown colder. Colder, as if somewhere a door had been opened. ''I know it seems impossible but it's true. And even if he had to go the long way round Mr. Gadsby can't be far behind.''

There was a pause, in which they both seemed to be listening. Then Daisy said tightly, ''Better get the police. There's a telephone in the basement. Been there ever since I can remember although it's hardly ever used.'' She pointed. ''You go right across the hall and down the steps. I'll stay here and give the alarm if he comes.''

''Wouldn't it be better if we kept together?''

''And be caught unawares down below?'' Daisy's eyes roved. ''Wait a moment. I'll get one of the brass candlesticks to defend myself with.'' She marched away, her back rigidly upright.

Sara, without thinking much about it, stepped up to the figure in the niche and put out her hand to twitch the blue cloak into place. Instead she found herself standing stiffly staring.

One of the bits of looking glass—one that ordinarily would have been hidden under the cloak—seemed to shine, not with any reflection but, as it were, in its own right.

It was like a great drop of clear water. It was like a sliver of ice. A star a million light years away. It was cold—and yet fiery.

So that was why Mr. Gadsby had dissuaded them from examining the plaster figures when she and Alan had been here before. The diamond had to be somewhere, so why not here? Here, where Mr. Gadsby could admire it undisturbed?

Mr. Gadsby . . . ?

She dropped the hem of the frock and the little pieces of looking glass scraped together as it fell into place. Sara shivered and goose flesh sprang up on her arms as she turned away. It had sounded to her like the dry rattle of dead bones.

Daisy came back, brandishing one of the heavy candlesticks. ''There now, Miss Sara,'' she said with an anxious smile, "don't you fret. If Mr. Gadsby comes it'll not be us who'll suffer."

Sara hesitated. "Daisy, you're sure this is the best plan."

"Get on with you, miss!" Daisy waved her impatiently away. "There's no way to the basement but by going right across the hall and down the steps there. I'll be standing at the cross aisles. You'll hear me shout if anyone comes." She added grimly, "But don't you come tearing back. It's the police we want and we may want 'em quick."

Sara turned away. Then paused, hesitating. She thought she had heard a sound from beyond the heavy curtains, the very faintest of movements.

"Did you hear that?"

Daisy looked at her quickly. "You think someone came in?"

"Or has been here some time." Sara's voice was no more than a breath of sound.

They stood there, staring at each other while confidence seemed to die and fear creep in. They listened but neither rustle nor whisper of sound came from behind the curtains.

"Oh hurry, miss," said Daisy at last in an urgent voice.

When Sara had crossed the width of the hall she looked back. Daisy was still standing where she had left her. She appeared very small and ineffectual. She saw Sara looking her way and raised the candlestick in gallant acknowledgment.

The transition from the luxury of the chapel to the bleak desolation of the basement was abrupt and complete. The walls were unplastered. The steps down were of stone with an iron railing. The electric light bulb at the foot was unshaded and thickly coated with dust.

A creaking door shut off the basement from the stairs. Sara pushed it open and the light from the single light was enough to show her the dingy walls and a great pile of what she took at first to be packing cases but which she saw on closer inspection were the disused tanks from the aquarium, abandoned and left to dust and decay. They were piled roughly one on top of another down the centre of the basement from end to end.

Unshaded electric bulbs hung at intervals but Sara could not find the switch to turn them on, nor could she spare the time to look for it. "At least there're no rats," she told herself and stepped into the gloom.

Her feet whispered on the floor boards and she could hear her breath rasping in her throat. Deformed shadows spread their monstrous shapes upon the walls. Then what light there had been faded and there was, for company, only her own shadow, thin and spindly, going before her. That dwindled and vanished and she was quite alone. Not even Archie Slater's phantom form accompanied her.

By now her eyes had become accustomed to the gloom. She realised that a certain amount of light came in through the gratings outside. She could see that the glass tanks were covered with some sort of greenish mould—but only in part so that a distorted image of herself attended on her with an eerie suggestion that someone else was there, keeping pace, peering in from the other side.

And all the time her whole body seemed tense, straining to catch some cry from above that would tell her that Mr. Gadsby had stepped from behind the curtains. She was haunted too by an obsessive belief that somewhere in the labyrinth of shadow and piled tanks someone, or something, was watching her progress.

She came at last to the far end of the basement. There was a chair there and a small table on which stood the telephone, a local directory and a pad and pencil. Piles of folding chairs and some trestle tables stood against the walls. There was a door here, leading she knew not where.

She felt surprised to find that this end of the basement had been kept clean but there was no time to puzzle over the fact. She put her hand out to the telephone and then froze where she stood.

A sudden small sound had come from behind her. And louder than the sound was the conviction that she was not alone.

She thought suddenly of Daisy waiting unsuspecting in the chapel above. Of Alan coming in to look for her. She must warn them—but how? Her mind that had slithered crazily under the first shock now settled to an ice cold appraisal of her position.

Scream a warning? It would not carry as far. The telephone? It would be dashed from her hands before she could do more than lift the receiver.

There remained only the door. It might, at the least, offer her space to manoeuvre. At best, it might lead to the outside world.

Her mind made up she sprang forward, jerked it open. Saw there were stairs beyond and that a faint light came down. But it was not the light from outside in the fog. It came from one of the star-lamps burning in the chapel above.

She could see part of a pillar supporting the gallery. One of the winged beasts looked down. She recognised them with the stunned incredulity that precedes the realisation of disaster.

So that was it, she thought dully. There *had* been another explanation to the letter.

The murderer had not been Mr. Gadsby. It had not been Mr. Gadsby tracking her through the fog. It had been Daisy.

For a moment she seemed held in the timeless quality of a dream. The stairs and the chapel above had all the clarity of remembered objects seen in an abnormal moment.

And that moment nearly cost her her life.

She heard a rustle behind her. Felt a rush of air. Instinctively she ducked, half aware of Daisy's maniacal face close to her own and the glint of brass as the candlestick came down.

It missed her head but struck her shoulder. A stabbing pain seemed to shoot down her arm, then extend all over her entire body.

Fortunately for her the weight of the candlestick had caught Daisy off balance. Sara, dodging around her, was able to throw herself down and crawl rapidly into a space left between the last of the piled tanks.

As she drew her legs in, Daisy made a jab at them catching her shin bone with the edge of the candlestick.

Sara gave an involuntary scream of pain. She crawled further into her retreat. Between pain and nausea she might have been lost in sheer physical terror but for her anger. She felt it run through her veins like a tonic and a desperate determination to live filled her mind.

From where she crouched she could see Daisy's spindly legs and her neat shining shoes, like twin black beetles. She could hear her panting breath but she did not speak. Sara found it odd that she did not speak.

Something fell with a crash in the chapel above. Daisy gave a cry of alarm, a strange animal cry. The spindly legs, the shining shoes vanished from before the opening.

Alan! Sara thought in terror. Alan must be up there. She imagined that she screamed out a warning but the sound existed mostly in her own mind.

Abandoning the shelter of the empty tanks she began a slow painful crawl towards the stairs. Her arm, she thought dully, must be broken and one leg dragged painfully behind her.

Faintly, and as if it had to penetrate through layer upon layer of smothering cloth, she heard Daisy screaming abuse. Then there seemed other sounds, whether in or out of her head she could not decide. The air seemed to fill with a great roaring as if many feet pounded above her. Then everything went dark.

Sara, her whirling head resting on the stairs, had lost consciousness.

A quick reconnaissance had been enough to show Finch that, but for Magda Brooks and the three old ladies, No. 9 was empty. Now he was on his way to the Chapel of the Watchful People, going as fast as Protheroe's skill in the fog allowed. Fortunately this was considerable.

"I had a man watching Mr. Kardos but I feel certain that he's lost him before now," said Finch in his murmuring voice. Adding plaintively, "If only Superintendent Enderby had come out of his premature retirement."

Protheroe remarked, "I used to visit the aquarium a lot when I was a nipper. Found a way of opening one of the side doors by shaking it." He chuckled.

Slater said nothing. He knew now, beyond any doubt, that Finch had been right. He did want to get somewhere with Sara. To him her thin pale face had come to epitomise all beauty, all that was desirable. When he thought of her alone in the fog—or worse still, in the Chapel of the Watchful People, his whole stomach seemed knotted with fear.

Protheroe spoke again, his eyes still fixed on the road unwinding in short lengths before him. "Queer to think that the murderer was Mr. Gadsby all along."

Finch was surprised. "But it wasn't Mr. Gadsby. I realised that as soon as I heard he had openly attended Mrs. Harkness' funeral. It was Daisy. Daisy who came back secretly for the diamond and was seen arriving by Miss Millamont."

"But why didn't the old lady mention it at the time?"

"That was a class thing. Belonged in her day and age. Remember her saying over the telephone, 'One doesn't gossip, you understand.' She meant that one doesn't gossip about the doings of servants. Providing, of course, that they were not doing anything unbecoming to their station in life. Miss Millamont, with her small but assured income, her comfortable home, upheld, as far as possible, all the shibboleths of her youth."

Finch paused a moment, then added handsomely, "It's strange but I haven't yet fathomed what it was that reminded her, after five years, of Daisy's return." He was genuinely surprised at this lapse on his part.

Slater roused himself from black despondency to say, "I

think I can tell you that, sir. It was probably hearing Sara say, late last night, that Daisy had only missed one Revelation Day in thirty years and that was the year when Mrs. Harkness died. We were standing at the foot of the attic staircase at the time. Miss Millamont must have been out of her room and have overheard.''

"So it was on Revelation Day that Daisy came back? I suppose we might have guessed that. If anyone saw her she had her excuse all ready—but no one did see her—except screwball Miss Millamont. Daisy was able to steal the diamond and get away undetected.''

Said Protheroe suddenly, "We're almost there, sir.''

Almost! Slater felt his whole body cold with apprehension.

The car drew up. The three men sprang out. They tried the main door and found it locked.

Protheroe raced away and found another door. He shook and pressed it. After a moment there was a clanking sound and the door opened. They found themselves in a small lobby. A second door opened into the main body of the hall but over to one side. The place was unlighted except for a single golden star, glittering under the dome.

Something seemed to be going on high up under the roof. The light did not extend as far and it was difficult to see exactly what but the two C.I.D. men were afraid that Sara was concerned in it. They could hear someone screaming in a high animal voice and thought it must be Daisy.

Finch told Protheroe to find the light switches and turn them on. He and Slater ran down the side aisle towards the source of the noise.

The lights came on. Everything came vividly into view. The altar—if that's what it was. The velvet draped walls. A group of plaster figures and one which seemed to have fallen from its niche and everywhere the glitter and glow of brass and gilt.

They could see the gallery now, far up and dwarfed by distance. Alan Harkness was there. He was wearing dark jeans and a short black leather coat and appeared to be struggling to open the door which led onto the roof. He was impeded by Daisy who, scratching and clawing, seemed bent on damaging his good looks rather than on retrieving the diamond which neither man doubted was now in his possession.

Advancing upon them swiftly and surreptitiously was the stout figure of Istvan Kardos. When the lights came on he did not turn his head nor stop his stealthy progress yet Finch would have sworn that, for a second, his whole body stiffened, as if in acknowledgment of the meaning of that happening.

Now Alan had abandoned his attempt to get onto the roof. Daisy and he were engaged in an open battle in which she seemed to be gaining the advantage. He struck out at her but the blow was misjudged by reason of the blood flowing from a deep scratch over his eyebrow. He seized the railings and kicked her in the stomach. She fell back, bounced off Mr. Kardos and came again, winding her arms about him, forcing him back against the railings, whilst Kardos danced in and out on his toes like a referee at a boxing match. Screams, curses and what sounded like remonstrance and alarm in various foreign tongues, all mingled in one horrid cacophony of sound.

Finch had been shouting admonitions to them without much hope of any result. The railing against which the combatants strained and fought was, designedly, a high one. There was no fear that either of them would fall over.

Not, that was, as long as the railings held. Finch wondered whether it was his imagination or whether the great gold cross up aloft was beginning to sway.

"The cross is coming down," Slater shouted suddenly. "The railings may go with it."

"No time to get to them," cried Finch in answer. "We must try and break their fall."

They seized the heavy velvet covering from off the table. They dragged it forward to serve as a net, crying out futile warnings as they did so.

The great cross shook and quivered with every bump on the iron railing. It jerked suddenly. There was a rending and a cracking. The cross described an arc in the air, then swung out, taking some six or seven feet of railing with it.

Someone, Finch thought it must be Alan, gave a scream of terror. He and Daisy, still locked together, plunged downwards.

Kardos, dropping to his plump knees, made an ineffectual grab after the vanishing pair. There was another wrenching sound and the great cross, the length of iron railing still attached to it, followed, like a comet.

There was nothing anyone could do. All three struck the velvet table cover. The two detectives were drawn together by the force of the impact. The cover, with its triple burden, bumped on the floor like a well filled shrimping net.

There was a stunned and yet ominous silence. No sound came from within the velvet cover. No sound from the two men

who held it. No sound from the man who looked down through
the gap in the gallery railing. Nor from Protheroe, white faced
and staring.

Then Kardos was moving, light as a cat, along the quiver-
ing gallery towards the stairs. Finch and Slater stepped back,
away from each other, uncovering their catch.

First came the gilt cross and railings. Under it was Alan
Harkness still clutched in Daisy's fierce embrace and with the
back of his skull crushed in where the cross had struck it.

Daisy was still alive. She was conscious but only just. She
appeared to be in no pain. Finch fancied that her back was
broken.

She muttered something and he bent over to catch the
words.

"Be thou faithful unto death and I will give thee a crown of
life." She smiled, a thin triumphant smile, into his face.

He saw that she still wore the brooch with "Satisfied"
written on it in silver letters. Extraordinary as it appeared, it
seemed that that, even now, summed up her mental attitude.

"No sign of Miss Harkness," he said aloud, "but that
doesn't mean she isn't here. You want to look for her, Archie?"

Slater was on one knee going through Alan's pockets. He
was looking for the diamond. "No, sir," he said to Finch's
surprise. "You go." Tight lipped he bent again to his task.

"There's a basement below this, sir," said Protheroe. He
spoke unsteadily and his gaze was wild. "The stairs should be
somewhere about here."

He walked rather blindly away. He came to the opening to
the stairs and stood staring down. "She's here, sir," he cried.
He felt now completely unnerved. "Miss Harkness, sir—and
there's blood all over her."

Finch, with a sinking heart, pushed past him. To his relief
he found that Sara was only unconscious. Indeed as he reached
the foot of the stairs she moaned and moved a little as if she
were coming round. She was lying awkwardly. Blood had soaked
through her coat at the shoulder and there was a great raw gash
on her right leg.

"Nothing fatal there," Finch muttered thankfully a moment
later. He raised his voice "Protheroe, look round and see if you
can find anything that would do for a stretcher."

Protheroe made a great effort to appear calm. He came
blundering down the stairs and began hunting about. He was
soon back carrying the top of a trestle table. Very carefully the

two men laid Sara upon it. They carried her up the winding stairs into the chapel.

It was strangely quiet there. Slater stood, ramrod stiff and pale as a ghost, at the feet of the dead man. Although he was looking towards the stairs he did not move as the little cavalcade appeared. It was left to Kardos to hurry forward with cries of astonishment and dismay.

"Miss Harkness is not badly hurt," said Finch, "but I want her out of here before she regains consciousness and begins to enquire after that brother of hers."

"Ah, that young man! What dark secrets of his may still be waiting to be discovered," said Kardos, wagging his head.

It seemed to Finch that there was a peculiar significance in the Hungarian's voice but the man said nothing further and the detective did not press him. He recognised that Kardos would speak when he felt like it. And that would be when he judged that it would do him most good.

Finch looked across at his sergeant. "Archie, come here and take my place."

Slater moved forward stiffly.

"Did you get the diamond?"

"Yes, sir." Slater felt in his pocket. He passed Finch what looked and felt like a ball of fine soft lawn. Opening it Finch saw that he held a long thin strip of material torn from the skirt of the statue. The diamond still attached to it by the gold thread embroidery.

There it lay, the cause of all the trouble. Brilliant, flawless, ice cold, and yet, with a strange radiance. No wonder it had been named the Lake of Fire. No wonder. . . .

He became aware that Protheroe was peering over his shoulder, staring in silent fascination. Kardos too, his eyes narrowed, his lips drawn into a straight hard line.

"D'you remember it?" Finch asked him.

"I had forgotten that it was so beautiful," said Kardos between his teeth. He closed his eyes for a moment as if the sight hurt him.

"Let's go," said Slater abruptly. Of them all he seemed the only one disinterested.

Protheroe, recalled to duty, took a firmer hold of his end of the table top. Finch stared after them. There had been, he thought, something distinctly peculiar about Archie's behaviour.

He put the diamond into an inner pocket and returned to the

basement. He telephoned to the police station and for an ambulance. Then he went back upstairs.

It was quieter than ever in the chapel. Kardos was standing where Archie Slater had stood but there the resemblance ceased. He was smoking a cigar, quite unperturbed by the company he kept, the coils of blue trailing upwards towards the dome, mingling with the writhing fog.

For all the ease of his attitude it passed through Finch's mind that he had been up to something. He dismissed it as unlikely. That wily gentleman would not do anything to further prejudice his precarious position.

There was no sound now from Daisy. Finch walked over to look at her. She was still alive but she was unconscious. He thought that her breathing had worsened but there was nothing he could do for her.

Looking about him the broad outline of what had taken place was soon clear.

Sara, her search for Daisy taking her to the chapel, followed by her brother, lured on some pretext into the basement and there attacked, the weapon used being the elegant but massive brass candlestick, later abandoned by Daisy at the foot of the gallery stairs.

Alan, by some means not yet apparent, made aware of the hiding place of the diamond, abandoning his sister to her fate and yet driven into a state of panic by the sounds rising from the basement. How otherwise explain why that heartless and calculating young man came to commit the folly of trying to obtain the stone by tearing out the piece of fabric to which it was attached, instead of easing it gently from the gold threads which held it? So bringing the statue crashing down and Daisy racing up from the basement to cut off his line of retreat and force him to try and escape by way of the roof.

Ironical to think that it had probably been this last treacherous act that had saved Sara's life. Not that it mattered any longer to Alan. Finch was not given to moralising but he could not but deplore the waste of a life that had seemed to hold every promise of success. A golden boy—and it had all ended here, in this freakish chapel. Daisy, too. Only the diamond, the cause of it all, went on unscathed, indestructible. Finch fancied he could feel it burning in his breast pocket.

He had a look at the other plaster figures. Grotesque really. Then he walked down the central aisle. The silent presence of the Hungarian irked him. What did he want up there, standing so quiet and still? So—watchfully?

Finch turned and saw the chapel in its entirety. It occurred to him that perhaps old Mr. Harkness had not been Mr. Gadsby's only patron after all. And that the art master might have been responsible for the brass and gilt with which the chapel was decorated.

It would explain his enthusiasm when showing the place to Sara. It would explain, too, how he had come to join the sect of the Watchful People in the first place; for how else could he get in to see his work? And how typical of the man that no one knew. . . .

Finch became aware once more of the rotund and yet somehow rather sinister figure on the platform. What *did* the fellow want? Dismissing Mr. Gadsby from his mind Finch walked back down the aisle to stand beside Kardos; to stare with him at the dead body of Alan Harkness.

His eyes took in the details.

The narrow feet in rubber soled shoes, the dark jeans, the dark leather coat, with the pale elegant hands looking even paler and more elegant as they protruded from the dark sleeves.

Finch saw that there was something light showing under the collar of the leather jacket. He bent forward to gain a closer view. Alan Harkness was wearing a pale blue nylon scarf round his neck but pushed back almost out of sight. A woman's evening scarf by the look of it, very fine, long and narrow.

"A strange scarf on such a day, eh?" It was Kardos who spoke, very softly and yet with a peculiar significance. "It reminds me of something." Adding, after a pause, "But of what I do not, at the moment, recall."

Finch's eyes were bleak. It reminded him of something too—and he had no difficulty at all in recalling what it was.

Chapter 14

Finch spent the next couple of hours as a bearer of bad news. He found that the council of the sect of Watchful People were sitting and broke to them the use to which their chapel had been put and the day's calamitous happening.

They were an unworldly, simple and comfortable body. Finch had an idea that his news had let in such a blast of the cold air of reality that it would prove as disintegrating to their company as would the expected end of the world.

Next he had visited the hospital. He had broken the news of her brother's death to Sara. Played down as far as possible, it had still been an ugly story. He had left untouched her belief that it had been Daisy behind her in the fog. Actually the police had traced the fisherman concerned and had from him a description of the person whom he had chased from the tunnel. His testimony had left no doubt but that it had been Alan.

Feeling depressed and a little weary he went on to the police station. There he found the Chief Constable. They were joined a moment later by Superintendent Enderby. Like Finch he was tired and depressed and looked it. He sank into a chair and wiped the perspiration from his forehead. It might have been July and not January.

"She's dead—Daisy Apps," he said heavily. "House surgeon was only surprised she'd lived as long. Had a broken back. Suspected internal injuries as well." He looked from the Chief Constable to Finch in a weary way. "Extraordinary woman. Know what she told me?"

"Of course not," snapped the Chief Constable before Finch, who could have made a good guess at part of it, had time to answer.

"She said—and when I say that I mean she sort of mouthed it at me in a thin kind of whistling voice. And her eyes had sunk

154

right in. It was like someone staring up out of a hole. Pretty ghastly really but she was determined to tell me the whole story—and with her voice dwindling the whole time and the doctor pumping stuff into her to keep her going.''

Again Enderby paused to wipe the perspiration from his forehead and now neither of his hearers interrupted him.

''She said that Mrs. Harkness had enjoyed talking to her about her past life but that she had always maintained that she'd had to sell all her jewellery to live. It was quite by chance that Daisy, herself unnoticed, saw the Lake of Fire; Mrs. Harkness, thinking her out of the house, having taken it from a specially contrived hiding place in an old morocco jewel case. From that moment it exercised a fascination, the reason for which she only understood years later.''

''What did she mean by . . . ?''

Enderby's heavy voice went on as if the Chief Constable had not spoken. ''Shortly before Christmas Daisy decided to steal the diamond and vanish but here history repeated itself in reverse as it were. Mrs. Harkness, returning unexpectedly caught her in the act. She turned her out of the house then and then.

''A few days later Daisy wrote expressing a contrition she felt only so far as her dismissal had separated her from the diamond. When her ex-mistress wrote refusing her request all her affection for her turned to hatred. A few weeks later, as we know, Mrs. Harkness was killed in an accident and Daisy, realising from the letters she got, that no one at No. 9 knew of her disgrace, returned on the day of the funeral and took the diamond.

''Did she say why she came back?'' Enderby asked.

''She said that her sister was a proper nosey-parker and that she never felt safe there. She was getting pretty weak by now so she jumped the matter of her return to No. 9. The next thing she said was that she never meant to cause Mrs. Winfield's death. Said the old lady went for her suddenly in the lift about her possession of the diamond and that, in consequence, she lost her temper. She was terribly upset afterwards and was praying about it when a Voice spoke to her. . . .''

''What?'' The Chief Constable's face froze between distaste and incredulity.

''That's what she said,'' the Superintendent spoke doggedly. ''Said she'd been guided to take the stone to the chapel and hide it there. Furthermore the Voice told her that she had been appointed its guardian. And that was why she had had to kill Mr.

McGee and later Mr. Carron. The Voice had said . . ." His own voice trailed away.

"Well? Go on, man!" The Chief Constable's eyes were hard.

"According to her the Voice said, 'I will have sacrifices.' "

"And then?"

"And then," said Enderby faintly, "she died. Died with a self-satisfied smirk on her face. I can tell you it made my blood run cold."

The Chief Constable threw himself impatiently back in his chair. "So now we shall never be able to fill in the blanks. Not very satisfactory, is it?"

"The only blanks surely are those concerning the death of her first two victims," said Finch. Adding thoughtfully, "From the maid's dying statement it seems that it was only Daisy's possession of the diamond that was questioned. Mrs. Winfield may never have heard the name of Tamara Lubova nor of the Lake of Fire. On the other hand how she came to know that Daisy had the stone does remain a mystery. Nor are we likely to find out whether Mr. McGee actually suspected Daisy or whether he was killed simply because he was too inquisitive for her peace of mind."

The Chief Constable had transferred his mean stare from the Superintendent to Finch. "And you can fill in the other blanks?"

Finch crossed one long leg over the other. "I think so, yes," he said in his soft drawling voice.

"Right. Then let us go back," said the Chief Constable ironically. "The telephone call, for instance, asking for Mr. Gadsby?" It was plain from his tone that he expected to trip up the Scotland Yard man, if not with that question, then with another.

"That was Daisy speaking probably through her handkerchief. Naturally enough, she was not anxious to be the one to find the body. When it came near the time for her to take tea up to the lounge and her crime was still undiscovered, she went outside to a telephone box. She asked for Mr. Gadsby, knowing that the first place anyone would look for him would be the hall." Adding with reluctant admiration, "She was as cool and resourceful a killer as any I have known and something of an actress."

"Yet your cool and resourceful killer panicked after seeing Kardos on the television screen."

"I think we were wrong there. It wasn't panic that led

Daisy to write that letter. She was God's chosen instrument and she set out to rebuke him. It was a pity from her point of view that the sudden break through of common-sense that led her to write that postscript didn't prevent her posting the letter.''

''When she knew Kardos was coming she got Sara Harkness to try and put him off. Not, I think, that she suffered much from anxiety—in spite of her display of hysterics. She had killed two people and got away with it. Obviously she felt herself to be under Divine Protection. And subsequent events must have con-firmed this belief. She was in the pantry and so heard Sara telephoning to Mr. Carron. She came downstairs in time to hear Miss Millamont's utterly inadequate identification over the tele-phone. That her subsequent attack on the old lady didn't quite come off probably surprised more than it alarmed her.''

Enderby smiled wryly. ''Frustrated by a fur hat.'' His smile broadened. ''She's going on nicely—Miss Millamont I mean. She isn't conscious yet but her general health has improved greatly.''

''That's splendid,'' said Finch. ''I always had a feeling that she was going to survive.''

''Did you suspect Daisy from the first?'' Enderby asked Finch.

''Not more than anyone else. I was concerned to identify Tamara Lubova, feeling that this would tell me who had the diamond and I was right. Daisy was clever enough to stick to the truth which was worse; for the only time she lied about the silver button she was found out. At the same time there were certain points about her behaviour that aroused my interest. For instance, when I met her first she spoke of her dead mistress as if she held a grudge against her. Then the way she suddenly changed her tune, as if she had realised that her show of enmity had been unwise, made me more interested still. Then again Daisy had been just as well situated as Mr. Gadsby to know that Mr. Carron was in the house and to first place, and then discover, the weapon in the sink. The attack on Miss Millamont ruled out certain people. . . .''

Enderby nodded. ''Madame Kosetti.'' He grinned. ''I can't see her getting in at that window without waking her intended victim.''

''And that goes for Mrs. McGee too. She had the agility, since her shoulder and arm muscles were abnormally developed, but she was clumsy. I couldn't see her climbing through the window without awakening Miss Millamont.'' Finch added, ''I never suspected Sara Harkness and I realised that her brother was responsible only for the smashing of the statuette of St. Nicholas and for the removal of Mrs. Harkness' papers from the attics. Papers which he subsequently tried to destroy in the boiler. Both useless acts since Daisy must have removed anything incriminating years ago.''

"Incidentally,'' said Enderby, "Protheroe tells me that he saw Daisy looking into the study when Miss Harkness was there but that, at the time, he thought nothing of it.''

"So Daisy, suspecting that Sara Harkness now knew the truth, went off quite happily to clean her chapel?'' said the Chief Constable with heavy sarcasm. "Or, are we to believe that she realised that Sara Harkness would suspect Mr. Gadsby?''

"You're forgetting Daisy's belief in her divine appointment. She couldn't very well kill her young mistress in a house as full of guests and policemen as was No. 9. But she could expect that Sara would follow her to the chapel to confront her with her suspicions before confiding them to anyone else.'' Finch frowned a little to him. "D'you know, I believe I'd have decided the same thing. That young woman had quite a passion for justice—for everyone but herself.''

"But Daisy couldn't have counted on the chapel being empty,'' Enderby objected. "Or could she?''

"That's the point. She could. It was kept locked for two days before the great day. In the first day a band of cleaners did the main body of the chapel. On the second day Daisy put the finishing touches, rubbing up the brasses and dusting the statues. No, the only danger of interruption was while she waited for Sara to arrive.''

"And you think that it was then that this singer fellow got in?''

"Yes, but I doubt whether he'll admit it, any more than he'll admit to being about last night and seeing the maidservant following Miss Millamont to the top floor.'' Finch added, "It was Alan Harkness, of course, who locked the outer door of the chapel. He didn't want any interruptions and, probably, having guessed that Daisy was the killer, hoped that she would dispose of his sister.''

"And then wasn't as hard-boiled as he had imagined. Shocking!'' Enderby wagged a mournful head. "Wonder how he came to find the diamond so easily?''

"His sister told me that she found and actually handled it. Alan must have seen this from his hiding place behind the curtains leading into the chapel but that's an idea I hope we shall be able to keep to ourselves." Finch rose to his feet. "That seems to be all—except for a last call at No. 9."

The Chief Constable stood up. He was glad to see the last of Finch. "I'm sorry not to have seen your sergeant to say goodbye," he remarked for something to say.

Finch was surprised. "Archie? That's very kind of you. I expect he's still at the hospital but I'll tell him what you said."

He took his leave of the Superintendent.

When he had gone the Chief Constable turned to Enderby. "No one told me his sergeant had been hurt."

Enderby smiled broadly. "He's not there as a patient. It seems he's fallen for Miss Harkness."

The Chief Constable stared. "A bit quick, isn't it?"

"Perhaps murder has the same effect as war," said Enderby tolerantly. "I can remember how quickly couples fell for each other then."

"And how quickly they parted company again," said the Chief Constable acidly.

Archie Slater, given permission by Finch to visit Sara, was filled not only with the doubts and fears proper to an unacknowledged lover, but by others peculiar to his position.

How could he court Sara when he was due to leave Seamarsh that very evening? How was he to see her again? Even convince her of the necessity? As he walked into the antiseptic atmosphere of the hospital the shadow and weight of his problem closed in on him, depressing him.

His first sight of her was enough to arouse in him a passion of tenderness. He would at that moment have performed prodigies of skill and valour on her behalf. Instead he stood tongue-tied, mutely staring.

She was so sad, so pale, so altogether frail looking and her eyes, shadowed by shock and grief, seemed to take up half her face.

Fortunately Sara's greeting could not have been better designed to break down any barriers. She stretched out her uninjured hand to him, then burst into tears.

By the time the storm had subsided she knew all that there was to know about his feelings. And he knew that he had made an excellent beginning, if no more.

They spoke sporadically—but not of Alan. She told him of her detestation of the diamond which had been the cause of so much tragedy. She could not bear to benefit in any way from its sale. The money must go to charity when the old ladies had been provided for. She spoke a little defensively, remembering her brother's dreams of wealth.

"Good—oh!" said Slater much relieved. "I shan't mind if you want to take up journalism again later on but I'm blowed if I want you to support me. As for the old ladies, I expect we can find someone to look after them."

"Oh yes. Let's do that," said Sara shuddering. "I don't feel I can ever go into the house again. At least, not for a long, long time."

"There's no need for you to go back there," declared Slater. "You can go straight from here to stay with my mother. She lives in Chiswick. She'll be delighted to have you. She's always saying she wished I'd meet a nice girl and get married."

"But I'm not a nice girl any longer," said Sara sadly. "Not in the sense your mother means."

"To me you're the nicest girl in the world," declared Slater stoutly. "And if you're thinking of the notoriety, the press can't get at you here. And, with Daisy dead, they'll have lost interest long before you're out of hospital."

Some time later Sara remembered something. "There was a piece of a letter in the pocket of my cardigan. . . ."

"That's all right. The hospital authorities found it and turned it over to my chief."

Sara sighed, turning her head restlessly on the pillow. "I realise now that old Mrs. Harkness was going to be reminded of Daisy because of the curtains and all the other things she had mended but there's still that bit about Hollodale—as Mr. Gadsby always called it. He found the old spelling in one of his books, Brook's Gazetteer, published in 1805."

Slater grinned. "The pernickety old gentleman."

"Well, then?"

Slater's grin broadened. "To my low mind it seemed that quite a different place was meant." Adding teasingly, "Not to mention that Mr. Gadsby's Hollodale is a river and one can't stay *in* a river. At least, that's been my experience."

"But what place did you think of?"

"Why, my silly sweet, Holloway of course. The prison for women. The letter probably went something like this. 'So stay away or you'll find yourself in Holloway after all.' "

The faintest of smiles lighted Sara's pale face. "You're clever," she said with conviction.

Slater sobered abruptly. "Clever enough to earn my living

in some other way? I mean—I might decide to resign from the police."

"Might you?" Sara stared at him wonderingly, trying to visualize him in some other occupation. "Somehow I can't imagine it."

Slater could not imagine it either. Not that he regretted what he had done, for how could Sara make anything of her life if she had to know what he knew.

Said Sara sagely, "I expect your Inspector will have something to say about it."

"So do I," said Slater ruefully—and somehow the thought of that bland resourceful man cheered him up.

With the discovery of the identity of the killer a great cloud seemed to be lifted from the house in Belmont Square. Difficulties that might have seemed insurmountable proved to be nothing of the sort, mainly because of Magda's initiative.

She went to see her late uncle's two maidservants and asked them if they would take charge of No. 9, if only temporarily.

They were middle aged, hard-working and kindly women and the thought of fulfilling a need appealed to them. Besides they had been attached to Mr. Carron and were glad of the distraction and of the prospect of having something to do. Although no one realised it at the time, they had assumed a responsibility that was to be theirs for the rest of their lives.

Magda, having settled things to her satisfaction and with her usual competence, went back to No. 9 to arrange for a passage to South Africa. With so much of death around her she was anxious now for the freedom to begin a new life.

To the three remaining old ladies, once assured that Sara was not badly hurt, the happening at the Chapel of the Watchful People seemed altogether satisfactory. The diamond had been recovered. Sara would be rich. Rich enough to provide for their future. They were too old to be anything but self-centred. Their anxieties, they felt, were at an end. They wasted no pity on Daisy or Alan.

Even Mr. Gadsby was happy. More sensitive than the old ladies, he had been overwhelmed by the knowledge that the cross he had designed had taken a human life—even one as useless as that of Alan Harkness. He would never willingly enter the chapel again—the chapel where he had spent so much time since the death of his dog.

"I'm just an ineffectual old man," he told himself sadly.

Then it had occurred to him that it was time he replaced Ajax. Thinking of all the dogs at the Battersea Home from which he could make a choice, he had cheered up considerably. It would be good to have a constant and devoted companion once more. And if anyone objected, he told himself belligerently, he would be quite willing to retire again to the Highlands.

Septimus Finch noticed the difference in the atmosphere as soon as he stepped into the hall. The uniformed police had gone. He could hear Madame Kosetti's voice coming from the lounge.

". . . and that was how this elderly, conventional lawyer, for love of a woman, became the knight errant, the lion heart," it was saying. "We laugh, Tamara and I, but it is, you understand, the laughter with tears. Then he die and we do not like that as well. In his will he has forgotten us and our needs. . . ."

She looked up and saw Finch in the doorway. It reminded her that here was someone who, like the late Mr. Harkness, knew the secret of her wealth. Her eyes glinted fire at him but her voice continued smoothly and without change. "Need, not of money, you understand, but of some little memento we could treasure. Something to show that he had had an affection for us, Madame Rakosi and myself."

Finch's quick eye took in the company. Magda Brooks, a quieter and somehow more restful Magda, the three old ladies sitting comfortably before the fire, Mr. Gadsby, shadowy in the background. The well laid tea tray, the cakes and hot scones. The vases full of flowers.

"We're having a little celebration," said Magda, shaking hands. "I hope it isn't dreadful of us."

"I was just going to tell how I had planned to pay Sara a pound more for my board," Madame Kosetti told Finch. Adding comfortably, "But now, of course, there will be no need."

Finch still had a few questions to ask. They were answered quite cheerfully and obviously were accompanied by no feeling of guilt. Indeed Mrs. Bradshaw seemed almost proud as she admitted to creeping along the coping and removing the photograph from Miss Millamont's room.

"Vera Millamont had told us of your interview with her and so we realised the necessity," she explained.

Finch did not bother to point out the enormity of her behaviour. He knew that it would be a waste of breath. Instead he asked why it was that no one in Seamarsh had been able to identify Mrs. Harkness with Tamara Lubova.

"After all," he ended, "she was only in her forties when she came here as a bride. There was this red hair as well as the retroussé nose."

"After the death of her protector, the archduke, Tamara had much trouble," Madame Kosetti explained. "She had to fly from Austria. It was then that she bleached her hair and went to live in Berlin. And it was there that she met the English doctor. He was with the Army of Occupation. A good man but of a dullness. . . ." She rolled her eyes in a parody of horror.

"And her nose? Was it plastic surgery which altered its shape?" Finch asked curiously.

Madame Kosetti shook with laughter. "It was a Torquay omnibus. It was a wet day and Tamara slipped whilst going to the top. She broke her nose on the steps. And, although it was reset, it was not, you understand, the same nose."

Finch felt defrauded. All the extraordinary contingencies he had conjured up and the truth had been a municipal bus allied to a wet day. "Didn't Miss Millamont ever connect her photograph with the woman she had seen in Vienna?"

"Nevair!" Madame Kosetti made the most of the rolling negative. "In the photograph Tamara was mature. Besides, constant bleaching had spoilt her hair. It was no longer a crowning glory. And with her new nose she was no more the beauty. Nice looking, yes. But not the beauty. It was no wonder she preferred to be remembered as she was."

"One more question. When did you and Mrs. Bradshaw first hear of the Lake of Fire?"

"I heard of it when it was given to that naughty Tamara. Such a scandal it made. Freda Bradshaw did not hear of it until Maud here told us of Tamara's dying confidence."

"And when was that?"

"After she had seen Istvan Kardos through the window of some house in Seamarsh," said Mrs. Bradshaw.

Madame Kosetti laughed. "Poor Maud! To hear of its beauty and its value was too much for her. Such tears you never did see."

None of the three had been able to think of a way of discovering the thief, still less of recovering the jewel. There had been so many people in and out of the house at the time of the funeral, the diamond might have been anywhere. Only with the death of Mr. Carron had they realised that the stone must still be in the house. They admitted that if they had talked the matter over with Vera Millamont they might have realised Daisy's guilt.

As it was they had decided that the great thing was to keep secret their knowledge of the identity of Tamara Lubova.

"If the stone had been found we could have claimed it on Sara's behalf," Madame Kosetti declared. "As it was our great wish was that she should not know that it was hers for fear harm came to her."

"And how right we were," said Mrs. Bradshaw complacently.

Mrs. McGee nodded her head. "As long as she knew nothing she was safe."

Again Finch held his peace, aware of the slightly ironical expression on Magda Brooks' face. Misguided the old ladies had been but they had meant well. They had been moved by unselfishness. Undeterred by danger. They had not confided in Sara for her own sake. Some time she might like to know that.

"One thing still puzzles me," said Finch. "Why did Tamara change her name to Millicent?"

The old ladies looked blank but Mr. Gadsby gave a slight cough. "The Victorian language of names," he explained. "I blame myself that I did not recognise it at once. Millicent means the sweet singer."

"That," said Madame Kosetti, "must have been the invention of the doctor, the so dull and worthy man from Torquay."

Finch took his leave of them. Now there was only Mr. Kardos to interview. As he went upstairs he felt his heart beating a little faster at the thought—not of seeing the Hungarian but of what he had to tell.

Mr. Kardos was in his vast and icy barn of a bedroom. Sitting in the little pool of warmth created by the electric fire. Beside him stood an incongruous object, a cheap fibre suitcase such as Finch had once postulated as waiting for its new owner in some railway cloakroom.

He was dressed ready to leave, even to his hat and overcoat. At the same time he gave the impression of waiting for someone. He sat relaxed, his short legs and neat small feet stretched out to the warmth. He was smoking a cigar with every appearance of enjoyment and there was a second chair drawn up to the fire.

"So you have come," he said, as though they had had an appointment. "Please be seated. A cigar? You should cultivate the habit. So much better for the health than a cigarette."

"So much more expensive," Finch retorted.

Kardos gave him a hard quick glance. "In some countries I

might take that as an invitation to press on you a hundred or so—cigars. Or something more valuable.''

Finch was amused. ''But this, of course, is England,'' he said smoothly, taking the second chair. ''What I really came round for,'' he added, ''was to ask you why and when you arrived at the Chapel of the Watchful People?''

''Why?'' Kardos smiled blandly. ''You ask me why I visited the chapel? I will tell you. It was idle curiosity. At first I couldn't find the place. But then I couldn't find any hotel either, so I had nowhere to go to get out of that fog and a singer learns to dread its cold touch.'' He shuddered affectedly. ''So,'' he smiled again, ''I must persevere. And at last I found the chapel. It was warm. I could see at once that much money had been spent. I congratulated myself. Then I heard a crash in the distance. I was curious, you understand. I ran and drew back the curtain and looked through.''

Far more graphic than his words had been the expression that flitted across the frog-face. Relief at having come in out of the fog. Pleasant surprise at the warmth and luxury. Then surprise without the pleasure. He drew back the curtains and astonishment seized him.

''There I saw Alan Harkness, far away where a single lamp burned. He is bending over a fallen statue. He seems to be trying to tear its skirt. I cannot understand. Is he mad I ask myself? Then Daisy appears. He runs for the gallery stairs. He is wise for plainly this one *is* out of her mind. She follows him, so respectable looking in her dark frock but screaming such things as might have originated on the waterfront of Marseilles.

''She is gaining on the young man. He turns. He tries to kick her down the stairs. Not a very gentlemanly thing to do I think, Inspector. Then I see his intention. There is a door out onto the roof and, no doubt, some sort of fire escape as laid down by your excellent byelaws. But alas!'' Kardos' face wrinkled into a mask of sorrow. ''He cannot get the door to open.''

He paused to draw on his cigar. When he spoke it was briskly—in quite a different tone. ''All this time, you understand, I have been approaching, drawn by my curiosity. How will it end I ask myself? Then I think I know. It will end badly. That madwoman has caught up with him. She attacks him. He is strong but she is stronger. I break into a run. And, Inspector, you will agree that I am built for the armchair, or the couch, but not for running. But I run now. I must do what I can to save

him. I, a fat old man, short of breath and not in the best of
health.''

"You make me cry," said Finch sadly.

Said Kardos simply, "It is, I think, a matter for tears. Up
the stairs I go. I plan a surprise—on tiptoe but it is no good. The
rail goes. They fall, the pair of them, murderer and victim. By
this time you too have arrived. I grab at them but in vain. You
hold out the net. But the cross and the iron railing fall down on
them. I know then that all is over. That handsome young man,
possibly the woman too, is dead.

"I turn to make my way down. The gallery shakes like
aspic jelly. I walk on tiptoe again but this time I hold my breath.
Presently I too reach the floor—but I am still alive. And now I
have told you everything and," he added in a voice suddenly
hard, "now I go home."

"Perhaps not quite everything. We found the door of the
chapel locked."

"Not locked. Stuck perhaps." Kardos was bland. "You
were in too much of a hurry."

"Or you, perhaps, arrived a great deal earlier than you
said."

"Inspector!" Kardos' reproach was a purr. He added thoughtfully, "But you are right in one way. There is one thing I have
not told you. Your sergeant now."

"Archie Slater?" So here it comes, Finch thought. His
expression did not change. It remained bland as a gambler's
although his thoughts raced.

Kardos smiled, not pleasantly. "That is the one. He rear-
ranged the evidence."

"In what way?"

"He took from the dead man's pocket a thin pale blue scarf,
twisted and in the form of a running noose. It isn't a nice thing
to find—this thug's weapon. And whom had he meant to attack?
The maid, Daisy? He made no attempt on her even when she
provoked him. His sister then—this young woman who was
suddenly to become rich? Your sergeant must have thought so,
for he took the scarf, undid the noose and put it round the young
man's neck."

So that was it! No wonder the scarf had looked so uncom-
monly like a rope. And Slater had moved it. The damned young
fool. Just wait until I get him alone, Finch thought. He stared at
Kardos, a formidable gaze with nothing sleepy about it. "Are
you, by any chance, about to try and drive a bargain?"

"Me? A bargain?" Kardos looked astounded, hurt. "No, no. I tell you only because perhaps it is better that I say nothing about this little incident. It is not in my character, you understand, to inflict unnecessary pain." He made a wide gesture. His expression was noble and benign. He seemed to be evoking the phantoms of numerous past good deeds.

Finch looked at him coldly. "All the evidence, including what you have just told me, will have to go to the Public Prosecutor for his consideration." His mind was already busy on that report. *"Under the circumstances and seeing that both the protagonists were dead, I thought it best to order the removal of the scarf from the pocket of the deceased. . . ."* "I can't, of course, say what he will decide but it is quite possible that you will hear nothing further although you will of course, have to appear at the inquest." His projected action was not as noble as it seemed. With the case virtually closed he would meet with no more than a formal rebuke. But, on the other hand, it would have been a serious matter for a young man of Slater's age and rank.

"I quite understand," said Kardos—as indeed he did. He sat smiling to himself. Then he burst out laughing. "Ah, what a denouement! Up there, under the roof. You English have a saying to fit every case. And now I say it. That young man, Alan Harkness, he fell off the deep end, no?"

He took up the cheap little suitcase. He shook hands with a flourish, still laughing so that all his gold teeth were visible, and went from the room.

Left to himself Finch sat where he was, sighing. "And there goes a very naughty old foreigner," he murmured aloud. "He began the case and he's ended it."

He thought of Sara and Archie and was not so sure that the affair could be said to have an ending. Because of it those two would marry. Sara would learn to live with all she need know of her brother's intentions. In time she would come to remember only his good points. In time she would have children of her own—and probably he, Finch, would be asked to be godfather.

"Life's a rummy business," he mused aloud.

The habit of moralising seemed to be growing on him.

ABOUT THE AUTHOR

MARGARET ERSKINE has written over a dozen mystery novels in the classical tradition—carefully shaped and plotted and highly literate. The Erskines are a Lowland Scots family connected with the Stuarts by many inter-marriages and, from Bannockburn to Culloden, they fought on every battlefield of Scotland. Miss Erskine was educated by governesses and the vast resources of her father's library in South Devon. She now lives in London.

"THE BEST POPULAR NOVEL TO BE PUBLISHED IN AMERICA SINCE *THE GODFATHER.*"
—Stephen King

RED DRAGON

by Thomas Harris, author of BLACK SUNDAY

If you never thought a book could make you quake with fear, prepare yourself for RED DRAGON. For in its pages, you will meet a human monster, a tortured being driven by a force he cannot contain, who pleasures in viciously murdering happy families. When you discover how he chooses his victims, you will never feel safe again.

Buy this book at your local bookstore or use this handy coupon for ordering:

Inside Boston Doctor's Hospital, patients are dying.
No one knows why,
No one but . . .

THE SISTERHOOD

Nurses bound together in mercy. Pledged to end human suffering. Sworn to absolute secrecy. But, within the Sisterhood, evil blooms. Under the white glare of the operating room, patients survive the surgeon's knife. Then, in the dark hollow silence of the nighttime hospital, they die. Suddenly, inexplicably, horribly. No one knows why. No one but the Sisterhood.

One man, a tough, bright doctor, risks his career, his very life, to unmask the terrifying mystery. One woman, a beautiful and dedicated young nurse, unknowingly holds the answer. Together they will discover that no one is safe from . . .

THE SISTERHOOD

A Novel by
MICHAEL PALMER

"Compassion turns to terror . . . Riveting reading, I couldn't put it down."

—V. C. Andrews, author of *Flowers in the Attic*